WORTH
THE
WAIT

Praise for "Worth the Wait"

"This is in fact a very delightful coming-of-age story, fast-paced, natural and racy in style." – Diana

"The characters and the story were so well-written and realistic and I was totally sucked in!" – Abbi

"An excellently written portrayal of growing faith." – Paige

"I was sucked into the story. I laughed, cried and got mad along with Ellie as she learned that being a Christian doesn't mean that you will have a perfect life. I thoroughly enjoyed it!" -- Cindy

WORTH THE WAIT

Waltham Academy, Book One

By Laura Jackson

Cover design by Jenny Zemanek of Seedlings Design Studio.

Scripture quoted by permission from THE HOLY BIBLE: NEW INTERNATIONAL VERSION®. NIV®. Copyright © 1973, 1978, 1984 by Biblica. All rights reserved worldwide.

Scripture quoted from The King James Version is in the public domain.

Publisher's Note: This novel is a work of fiction. Names, characters, places, and incidents are either products of the author's imagination or used fictitiously. All characters are fictional, and any similarity to people living or dead is purely coincidental.

ISBN 978-1539068785 (paperback)

Printed in the United States of America

To my sister, Jeanelle.
The first day I started writing a book, you said,
"When this gets published..." instead of "if this gets published."
Thanks for believing.

ACKNOWLEDGMENTS

Thanks to Lynellen Perry for taking a chance on a newbie. I'm thankful for your vision.

Thanks to Betsy St. Amant for your advice and direction.

Becky Miller, your editing made this book publishable.

Thanks, Mom, for tearing up my story in the way only English teachers can and your unwavering support of me.

And most of all, Jesus. Your plan is definitely worth the wait.

1

Ellie counted the minutes until she could wrap her arms around Dylan's neck. Seventy-one days apart was seventy days too many. She checked her phone to see if he had replied to her text to pick her up before school, but there was nothing new. The last few weeks, he hadn't called at all, only sending a text here and there. And he hadn't greeted her at the airport last night when she arrived home from the summer in Nantucket Bay visiting her aunt. *One glimpse into his deep blue eyes, and I'll know if everything is the same between us.*

After straightening her hair again with the flat iron, she sighed and stretched. She'd spent the last hour and a half taming her naturally curly blonde hair into the smooth, sleek style that Dylan preferred. The first time she had straightened her hair, Dylan had commented that she was hot, so she didn't mind the time it took to look nice for him even though her curls made her stand out in a sea of girls with straight-as-a-board hair. If only she could wear something besides the school uniform. Lip gloss finished her morning make-up routine. How big would the smile on Dylan's face be when he picked her up in twelve minutes? If he picked her up. But he had done so every day since he got his license, so why should today be any different?

"Eleanor Rebecca Lansing, hurry up! You need to eat breakfast, and I want to get a picture of you on your first day of senior year." Her mother's heels echoed on the hardwood floor downstairs.

Grabbing her bag, Ellie hurried down the stairs. Her mom was posed like a paparazzo ready to pounce. Her sweet but smothering mom captured every life event with photos, and she had the scrapbooks to prove it.

"Is my hair okay? Dylan hasn't seen me in months, and I want to look good."

"Perfect as always. Say cheese." Ellie smiled for the camera. "I can't believe you're growing up so fast. It was just yesterday...."

Ellie gave her mom a hug as she started a jog down memory lane.

She checked her phone again. No message. She paced the living room. *Come on, Dylan! What's going on?*

"Nick, get down here too!" Her mom stood at the bottom of the stairs, shaking her head. "I'll bet your brother is still asleep."

Ellie's mom kept yelling until Nick finally clomped downstairs, goofy as ever. His rumpled pants and half-in, half-out shirt weren't going to meet their mom's J. Crew standards. Ellie braced herself for a battle of wills. "Come here and let me fix your hair at least."

"Knock it off, Mom. I don't know why school starts on a Thursday. Can't we just go Monday?" Nick rolled his eyes but tucked in his shirt.

How could Nick be such a slob? He certainly wasn't like her, though she had to give him credit for being his own man. *Poor clueless guy.* He would start to care about his appearance as soon as a girl came into the picture. The arguing over Nick's hair and the school board's decision for the start of school continued until Nick shut the bathroom door. *No wonder he sent me all those texts this summer, begging me to come home before Mom drove him crazy.*

A car door slammed. That had to be Dylan. Ellie took a deep breath, smoothed her hair, and ran to greet him in the driveway. His wide grin swept away her worries. His eyes, the color of Nantucket Bay on a clear day, drew her closer. "I've missed you so much, Dylan."

"Ellie." Dylan wrapped her in his arms and leaned back against his car door. She inhaled the familiar spice of his cologne. He bent down and brought his lips to hers. As the kiss deepened, he inched her shirt up and caressed the skin of her back. His fingertips were hot as his lips nibbled toward her ear.

"Careful, my mom will see." Ellie's cheeks grew hot and she pulled away, tugging her shirt back into place. Intertwining her fingers with his, she pulled him toward the house. *I guess he did miss me as much as I missed him.*

"Your mom has been planning our wedding since we were born, so I'm sure she wouldn't care. Relax a little, Ellie." He snuck in one more kiss before opening the front door for her.

"Hey, Mrs. L.!" Dylan walked into her mom's embrace.

"It's so good to see you. Linda talked nonstop about how busy you were this summer. Your hair looks even blonder from the sun." She smiled as she picked up her camera from the hall table. "Summer must have been good to you."

"It would've been better if Ellie had been here, but it was good." Dylan stepped back to Ellie and twirled a strand of her hair.

Nick stalked out of the downstairs bathroom a little more presentable than before but wearing a scowl. "How come you didn't come by to shoot some hoops this summer like you promised, Dylan? I texted you like ten times."

"Man, I'm sorry, but football training was hectic, and working as a lifeguard wore me out. I'll make it up to you, dude." Dylan reached for a fist bump, but Nick crossed his arms.

"Whatever, *dude*. We've played basketball every week forever, but this summer you were too busy?"

"Nicholas, there's no reason to be rude to Dylan. When you get to high school, you'll see how rigorous football training can be. After all, he's working to earn a scholarship to a major university." Her mother patted Dylan on the back, and Ellie smiled.

I'm so lucky to be one of the few girls whose mom loves her daughter's choice in boyfriends.

"Maybe you'd rather have him as a son than me." Nicholas glared.

"Well, at least he's presentable." Ellie's mom motioned everyone to the fireplace.

Ellie stepped in front of Nick. "Appearance isn't everything, Mom. I hear eighth grade girls like the casual look on boys these days."

Nick raised his eyebrows at his sister as if to say thanks.

Giving Ellie a kiss on the head, Dylan draped his arm around her shoulder as her mom took their last "first day of school" photo. He murmured in her ear, "It was a weird summer without you. Just not the same."

"Two months was way too long. I've missed you so much. Why'd you stop calling?"

"I'm here now." He ran his fingers down her hair and rested his hand on her waist. "The faster we finish, the faster we can be alone."

"Come on, kids. Let's see if we can do this shoot in under ten takes. Less talking, more smiling."

Ellie forced a smile and turned back to her mom. What had changed?

When her mom was finally satisfied with their pictures, they moved to the front porch for a quick breakfast. "You didn't call much the last month I was gone. I didn't know what to think. Then Nick says you didn't hang out with him like you promised. That's not like you." Dylan had often raved about how lucky Ellie was to have a little brother instead of a sister. Ellie offered to trade siblings, but neither set of parents went for the idea.

"Just busy training for football. I have to have my best season if I want a scholarship."

Ellie took a sip of orange juice. "I thought maybe you were still mad about what happened before I left."

Dylan leaned back in his chair and sighed. "Let it go. We fought. We made up. Move on."

Except it hadn't been a simple argument. He had pushed her further than she wanted to go, and she'd had enough of his pushing. Why'd he refuse to talk about it?

The orange juice curdled in her stomach. Ellie put her fork down and stared down the street where the elementary kids from the neighborhood public school were waiting for the bus. Dylan ate in silence.

When they brought their plates in a few minutes later, he stood behind her at the sink and wrapped his arms around her. "Don't be mad. It was just strange without you. I missed you, and I love you." He turned her around and kissed her cheek.

Tucking her head in his embrace as they walked to his car, Ellie breathed him in and relaxed. She was back, he was still crazy about her, and her senior year would be just as she always dreamed.

Ellie grinned at Dylan as they pulled into the parking lot of Waltham Christian Academy on the outskirts of downtown. "Can you believe we're seniors? We've got our last homecoming, the big mission trip, senior class trip, and prom. It's going to be the best year ever."

"On top of the world, baby. It's going to be amazing. Me the quarterback and you a cheerleader. Like something out of those stupid romance novels you read." Dylan unbuckled his seat belt and leaned in for another kiss. "You're so beautiful."

Ellie frowned at his jab at her sappy love story addiction but leaned into his embrace so she could soak up every moment of her senior year, starting with this one.

"Dylan!" A loud rap on the window ended the moment. Outside stood four of his teammates. "Hurry up, man."

"See you later, Ellie. It's time for football talk." Ellie and Dylan got out of the car. The guys gave each other half-hug, half-slaps on the backs. James, a thick-necked linebacker chest-bumped Dylan, who stumbled backwards. Xavier caught Dylan's arm and kept him from hitting the ground.

"Hey, James. The other team isn't going to lay a hit on our QB, so don't think you can get your shot now." They laughed as they headed to the gym.

"Duty calls." Dylan pecked Ellie's forehead, and the guys started whistling.

"Keep it clean, QB. You know Headmaster Phillips has spies out for any signs of 'public displays of affection' on campus," Xavier teased.

"See you in pre-calculus, my romance novel hero," Ellie whispered. She winked, then headed toward the picnic tables in the courtyard that separated the elementary from the middle and high school sections of campus. Cara had to be here somewhere.

"Ellie! Over here!" The girl waving at her had black hair cut in a short bob, not Cara's long hair that fell to the middle of her back. It seemed a lot of things had changed during her summer away. "You look so good. That two-month vacation did you right!"

"Your hair, Cara!" Ellie gave her best friend a hug.

"I know. I was bored without you. I'm so glad you're back. Let's compare schedules." Sitting down, Ellie picked up the latte Cara had waiting and pulled out her list of classes. "Ellie, we don't have one class together until cheer 8th period."

"Really? Maybe we can switch electives or something."

"I need to see Mrs. Santana about this today. Do you have any classes with Dylan?"

"Just one. Pre-calculus. Two months is a long time to be gone. I'm so behind on what everyone's been up to. Did you see Dylan much this summer?

"Not really. It was a little weird, actually." Cara stopped flipping through her backpack and looked up at Ellie. "Most of the usual group got together, but Dylan was always busy. Then he and Josh got into that fight, and I haven't seen him since. Josh refuses to talk about it aside from swearing that Dylan will get what's coming to him. He may be my twin, but it's clear I got all of the talking genes. Have you asked Dylan about it?"

Ellie nodded. "I just don't get why Dylan would give Josh a bloody lip now. Dylan didn't react when Josh humiliated me last spring. I asked Dylan about it a few times. He shrugged it off as guys goofing off and then rushed to get off the phone. But I didn't want to fight on the phone, so I gave up. He's been even more distant since then." She pasted on the smile her dad dubbed 'the cheer grin,' but Cara shot her a *this-isn't-over* glance.

"Eleanor Rebecca Lansing, you and Dylan are the perfect couple. He was just busy training for football. And whatever he and Josh fought about is apparently above our clearance level." Cara zipped up her bag and put it on her shoulder.

"You're right. You always are when you pull out the full name." Ellie stood and took another sip of coffee. "But I —."

"No more questions, Ellie. You and Dylan have been together since before you could form complete sentences. Even your parents are best friends. I have no idea why you're worried so much about your relationship. Did something happen you didn't tell me?" Cara stopped outside the front door.

"Well, right before I left, we got into a big fight."

Cara dragged her to the side of the school and whispered, "Okay, spill."

Ellie sighed and huddled close. "Whenever we were alone, he kept pushing for sex, but that last night, it was really bad. We fought about it, and I finally just asked him to take me home. But then the next morning he apologized and gave me the sweetest kiss goodbye at the airport. I thought things were back to normal. But maybe they weren't."

Cara opened her mouth to speak, but a squeal from Emma, the cheer captain, cut her off.

"Ellie! Cara! The team's back together." She ran up and pulled both girls into an embrace. Cara met Ellie's gaze and mouthed *later*.

"Reunited at last," Ellie sang as she hugged Emma. A huge grin split her face. While most people stereotyped cheerleaders as clueless, fickle attention seekers, Ellie believed most of her teammates were true friends who focused on encouraging not only the sports teams but also each other.

"It's obvious you didn't take any singing lessons over your summer away," Vanessa piped in as she joined the group hug.

"Oh, the newbie has jokes." Ellie pushed all thoughts of Dylan out of her mind and linked arms with Cara to open the doors on the last chapter of her fairy-tale high school experience.

2

Ellie grumbled at the English syllabus in front of her. "Homework on the first day of school. Group projects. Are you kidding me? I thought senior year was for goofing off."

"Perhaps you shouldn't have signed up for AP classes, Lansing."

Ellie turned. Joshua Martin had taken a seat next to her. Of course he'd be in the one class where she didn't have any other friends.

"My bad." Ellie faced the front. The pit of her stomach clenched up.

"Come on, Lansing, you can't let anyone see you without a smile. That wouldn't be very rah-rah of you." While Cara had bright blue eyes that made a striking contrast to her dark hair, her twin brother's brooding brown eyes often caught Ellie off guard. They seemed to see past her perky attitude to the feelings hidden behind the smile.

Glaring, Ellie faced him again. "What's your problem, Joshua?"

"No problem on my end, nothing at all. I just thought, now that it's our last year in this fishbowl, we could have a clean slate." Josh's glance darted around, never quite meeting hers.

"So, you start in on the cheerleading jokes to break the ice? After being one of my best friends for years, you humiliated me, didn't apologize, and then refused to talk to me about it. What did I ever do to deserve all that?"

"Nothing, Lansing. You did nothing at all. That's the point." Josh looked down at his paper and started doodling, ending the conversation.

"Whatever. That doesn't make any sense." After moving to a different seat, she spent the entire period resisting the urge to glare at him. The memory of Josh abandoning her on the stage near the end of their performance of *Romeo and Juliet* prevented her from hearing anything the teacher said.

The bell sounded. *Good thing the syllabus has the homework since I didn't hear a thing Ms. Hensley said.* Grabbing her notebook, she raced into the hallway, away from Josh. A few yards down the hall, she looked back. He leaned against the lockers, an odd expression on his face. The same one he had on stage when, as Romeo, he was supposed to confess his love for Juliet and kiss her. Instead, he'd said, "I can't do this, Lansing," and darted off, leaving Ellie alone under the bright stage lights, as red as the curtain that finally, mercifully closed.

Shaking her head, Ellie headed to the cafeteria to find Dylan, who would surely greet her with open arms and a ready kiss. Who needed a fictitious Romeo when a real one waited for her?

By the end of the day, Ellie had hugged almost every member of the senior class, been in twenty Instagram photos, starred in a few Snapchat videos, and worn out her cheek muscles. Finally, last period—cheer practice. As the squad ran a mile on the track around the football field, Ellie glanced toward

Dylan. His strong arms that held her tight. His shaggy blonde hair that fell in his eyes, always just shy of breaking the school's strict hair-length code. His wide smile that always cheered her up. His blue eyes that looked at her the way no one else did. How many girls could say they knew they had found the one God had for them when they were just kids? She was so lucky, or as her mom would insist, *blessed*, to have Dylan.

Ellie hurried to catch up to Cara, who was facing the field too. Would her independent "I don't need a man to be happy" friend admit to checking out a guy? She followed Cara's gaze as they rounded the corner of the track. Josh.

"What's he doing here?" Ellie's words came out in spurted breaths.

"Who? Josh?" Cara panted.

"Yeah, isn't that him?" Ellie didn't want to point since Josh seemed to be looking their way. "I thought he wasn't going out for football after the way the guys razzed him about trying out for the play and then running out like he did."

"Now that SBU has a football team, he'd like a shot at making their team. After all the teasing about the play died down, he decided he wasn't going to let anyone keep him from it."

"So, you two decided on Sugarland Baptist University for sure?"

"Josh has, and I want to stay close to him. That twin thing, you know."

"Yeah." Through the years, she had witnessed Cara and Josh have full conversations without talking, and their mom swore they had had their own language as babies.

"Why don't you go with us? Maybe it'll be like it was when we were kids. You know, building sandcastles at Galveston, doing flips on the trampoline, and having our Barbies marry Josh's GI Joe dolls."

"Don't start. You know I'm not going to spend four years away from Dylan. Two months was hard enough. No matter how many times you bring up Houston-area colleges, it's not going to happen. Not unless Dylan has a change of heart. And besides all that, I gave away all my Barbies a long time ago."

"Well, I won't fill out my roommate request just yet. Maybe you'll change your mind."

Ellie slowed to a walk as their five laps ended. She glanced back at Josh. *Good for him. I wish I could talk to Cara about what happened in English class.* Cara was on Ellie's side about the play fiasco, but that didn't change the fact that Josh was her twin, and she loved him.

"This summer I prayed that somehow the four of us would become friends again. I never liked the way we split up. " Cara began to stretch her legs while they waited for the other girls to finish running.

"Me either, but after the play, it's just so weird. He refused to talk to me about what happened, and now it seems too late to go back. I don't think we could ever clown around the way we used to." Ellie's breathing returned to normal, and she began stretching as the rest of the team discussed the upcoming homecoming dance.

The next afternoon, Ellie stretched out on a raft that floated her along the ripples in Connor Daniels' backyard pool. Twenty friends surrounded her, all talking over each other about their summers. How perfect. This yearly tradition had started back in second grade when all the moms wanted to get together to discuss who got what teacher and who would be homeroom mom. Even after the moms moved to brunch meetings, the kids kept the pool party. Today their conversations centered on who would be a starter on the football team, who would be in the homecoming court, and who was dating whom.

After an hour of soaking up sun and a game of water volleyball, Connor walked outside holding high a twenty-four-pack of beer, "Sometimes big brothers are worth the trouble!"

Ellie groaned. Last year had been the same thing. Someone whose parents weren't home hosted the party, and somebody found a college kid willing to buy some beer for fifty bucks. Why did these guys have to spoil a great party? Alcohol brought out the worst in Dylan. At last year's party, Dylan had pressured her to drink at parties and to have sex with him, even though he knew she had sworn to wait until she was married. She wasn't ready for another fight.

Dylan walked past her. She waved to catch his eye, but he didn't glance her way. He grabbed two beers. He opened one up, to the cheers of his friends, and took a long swig before holding up both cans. "Let's get this party started."

"So, it's senior year, Queen Ellie, how about you finally let go a little?" Connor had obviously had a few on the way back from picking up the beer. "I know Dylan would like you a little looser."

Ellie continued to float as if she hadn't heard him. She hadn't been voted to the homecoming court every year by getting into arguments with every drunk punk. But his words cut into her heart. Had Dylan been talking about her refusal to have sex with him?

"Everybody knows Little Miss Perfect won't drink, Connor. Don't try to talk to her into it. It'll just be a waste. But I'll take one." Lindsey Hamilton, a fellow cheerleader who thought it was cute to wear stilettos to a pool party, strutted up and placed her perfectly manicured hand on Connor's shoulder.

Tears filled Ellie's eyes. *I will not cry in front of all these people.* Everyone stared as she paddled the raft to the edge of the pool and climbed out. While Lindsey's words stung, they didn't hurt like seeing Dylan just watching it all. Not defending her.

Dylan finally walked over and stood between Connor and Ellie. "Back off, man."

Connor shrugged. "Whatever. I was just joking. She didn't have to take it so seriously." Everyone went back to their conversations, but for Ellie, it was too little too late.

She gathered up her things, searching for Cara as she started to leave. But Cara had left after an hour to be at the mall in time for her shift at a clothing boutique where they both worked. Ellie was out the side gate before Dylan could catch up to her.

"Where are you going, babe?" He reached out to grab her arm but got air instead.

"I'm leaving, Dylan. Isn't it obvious? Why didn't you stand up for me? How could you not say something when Connor said you would like it if I loosened up?" Ellie paced, her hands balled into fists.

"That's just Connor. He always ribs you about not drinking. You know that's what makes you special. You do what you think is right." A lock of her hair had fallen out of her messy bun, and Dylan brushed it out of her eyes.

Dylan's low voice was usually soothing. But right now it made her grind her teeth together. Too many things had been off since she'd gotten home, starting with Nick and ending with this.

"Yeah, he shouldn't have brought alcohol, but we're just here at his house. No one will be driving for hours." Dylan frowned.

"What did he mean by you wanting me to loosen up?" Ellie searched his eyes. *Please, God, don't let this end in another fight about sex. How many times do I have to say no?*

"Ellie, everyone knows about your commitment not to have sex until you get married. You talk about it every year in Bible class and any time the subject comes up in Sunday school. Guys say stuff. What difference does it make?" Dylan's eyes turned stormy. "Relax."

Ellie spun away. Her shoulders began to shake as the tears she'd been holding back finally escaped and trickled down her face. Dylan grabbed her arm, and she peered up at him.

"Don't be like this, so uptight like your mom. It's our senior year. I just want us to have a fun time, not argue." He brushed her tears away. "You're even beautiful when you're crying."

Ellie managed a smile. Here was the guy she had loved as long as she could remember. So what if he didn't rush to defend her like he used to? He had been talking to some teammates and not really paying attention. "It's okay. I shouldn't be so sensitive, but I'm going to head home. Be careful."

"Always. See you tomorrow." Dylan gave her a peck on the lips and headed back to the party before she even reached the end of the driveway.

She turned toward her house a few blocks over. And there was Josh, opening the door to his jeep. Just what she needed to make a bad afternoon even worse. *Was Josh at the party? Did he overhear Dylan and me?*

"Want a ride?" He offered without looking at her.

"Nah, I'm good. Need to clear my head." *I definitely don't want to be stuck in his jeep alone with him for even a few minutes. Talk about awkward.*

"It's getting dark. Be careful." Josh hesitated before getting in, like he had more to say.

"You know I have mad self-defense moves." Ellie struck a karate stance. Despite being in good shape, she was still only five three and no match for a guy like Josh.

"Maybe on a video game, but even then you suck, Lansing." Josh left his door open and walked toward Ellie. "Remember that time you couldn't figure out the buttons and kept running into a wall? It took you fifteen times to get it. I counted."

"Out loud, if I remember." Ellie reached toward him to slap his arm as she laughed, but then snatched her hand back as if she was about to touch a hot stove. Josh took a step back. Not sure what to do with her hands, she tried to stick her wayward hair back into its knot. "Well, thanks for the offer for a ride. I better get home."

"Yeah, that English syllabus awaits you." Josh got into his car.

"That's why I took AP classes." Ellie shouted back. For just a moment, their friendship peeked through the ice wall that surrounded her heart.

4

Saturday morning, Ellie awoke to a text from Dylan.

Come to your window.

He was standing on the lawn with a dozen long-stemmed red roses in his hand and a grin on his face. Her phone buzzed again.

Get dressed to get dirty.

Give me ten minutes to get ready. Ellie texted back.

She motioned him to go to the kitchen to wait for her. After a record-breaking shower, she dressed in black running shorts and a teal tank top. She darted downstairs and found her parents and Dylan in the kitchen eating pancakes and talking about the day's college football games. Her dad and Dylan's dad always spent a few hours each Saturday watching their *alma mater*, Ohio State University, play. Dylan and Nick often joined, while the girls spent the day shopping or hanging out. Sometimes it seemed as if the two families were already blended.

"What beautiful flowers Dylan brought you, Ellie." Her mom had put the bouquet in a vase on the kitchen counter.

"They're gorgeous. I love them." Ellie leaned down to give him a quick kiss on the forehead before walking over to smell the arrangement that belonged on a parade float. She smiled at the "Don't the roses get me more than that" look Dylan shot her, but it was all she could do with her overprotective father scrutinizing them.

"Well, Mr. and Mrs. L., it's been fun having breakfast, but I want to take Ellie somewhere before the football game starts at one. Are y'all coming over?" Dylan stretched before putting his plate in the sink.

"Wouldn't miss it, Son. Y'all have fun. Bring my girl back in one piece." Her father stood and followed them to the door. He gave Dylan the same warning every time they left. On their first date, Dylan confided that her dad had pulled him aside and told him when he said that, it meant one piece emotionally as well as physically.

Once in the car, Dylan leaned over and gave Ellie a kiss. "Sorry about last night. You're right. Connor's an idiot, and I should have been paying attention to what he said."

"Forgiven." Ellie ran her fingers through his hair as he backed out the car. "Where are we off to?" Dates with Dylan were never boring. One of their first dates had been to ride go-carts. There were only a handful of times they'd done the typical dinner and movie date.

"Well, I want to try something new. I heard about it from Xavier this summer, but it was too hot. It's called Frisbee golf." Dylan grinned like a boy who just got his first football.

"Sounds interesting. Do we try to fly miniature Frisbees into little holes in the ground?"

The rest of the way to the park, Dylan explained the rules. The object was to get your Frisbee into a metal basket in as few throws as possible. Ellie laughed. Dylan was in his element whenever there was a competition.

They parked near a group of about ten friends from school and a few people she didn't know, probably various dates. Xavier was there with his longtime girlfriend Amanda. Although Xavier played football with Dylan, Amanda wasn't the least bit interested in sports, focusing more on theatre. She and Ellie had become friends when Amanda had worked on the costumes and backdrops for *Romeo and Juliet*. Giving Amanda a quick hug, Ellie whispered, "Let's get on the same team."

"I'm glad you're here. You know I work hard to avoid the whole football crowd. It's good to see a familiar face."

"We're harmless. Over-caffeinated, but harmless." Ellie laughed. The group was splitting off into smaller teams to play together. Grabbing Amanda's arm, Ellie motioned to Dylan to pair up with Xavier. Cheer Captain Emma and her boyfriend Vincent, also a member of the football team, rounded out their group.

Two hours flew by, one laugh after another as Xavier, Vincent, and Dylan talked trash while the girls focused on making dance moves out of their tosses. When they finished the 18th hole, they collapsed and guzzled water. The sun, now high in the sky, had not gotten the memo that summer was over. The guys goaded Vincent, who had smoked them all in the game, getting him to reveal that he had been playing for a couple years with his family.

Leaning back on Dylan's sweaty chest, Ellie's heart beat in rhythm with his.

"That must be true love, letting him sweat on you like that." Amanda sat a few inches from Xavier as they rested under a tree. "We've been together almost two years, but I still don't want to hug him when he's sweaty."

"I'm a lucky guy." Dylan smiled as he checked his phone for what must have been the tenth time in the last hour. "She's sweating on me too, you know."

"We don't sweat, we glisten." Ellie pouted as if she were offended and tried to read what Dylan was typing, but he hit send and put it back in his pocket.

"That's right, and I try not to even do that." Emma had already wiped her face and was now applying lip gloss.

"Well, we're going to head out." Dylan stood up and pulled Ellie to her feet.

"It's been fun, girls. Next time we'll show the guys who's best." Ellie waved goodbye. Hand in hand, they strolled back to Dylan's car, riding home with the windows down and the music too loud to talk. When they got to her front door, Dylan gave her a long kiss.

"I'm going to watch the game with my dad and then head to the Astros' game with the rest of the offense. I'll talk to you tomorrow at church." Dylan turned, but she caught his arm.

"I love you, Dylan." Ellie stood up on her toes to kiss him again. She had been taller than him back in elementary school, but now at six feet tall, he dwarfed her. She watched at the door while he walked back to his car. His once lanky gait had grown into a confident swagger. He gave her a wink as he drove away. *I'm so lucky he's mine.*

She headed into the house, texting Cara to see if she was free to hang out before Ellie had to work at five. They had both signed up for the mission trip's planning committee, and Ellie had started writing her to-do list on the flight home from Nantucket. The school gave them the week after Christmas break to go on the traditional trip, hoping the project would spark a lifetime of giving back to the less fortunate.

Fundraising had begun freshman year to pay for travel expenses, and at the end of junior year, the class had voted to go to a small town in Sonora, Mexico, to help out at a church-run orphanage.

Now began the fun part—planning games, Bible lessons, and activities. Not to mention asking small businesses for donations of toys for the kids as well as other necessities for the orphanage. Ellie was in charge of coordinating the schedule and teams, which was perfect since she enjoyed making lists and organizing events.

As she and Cara brainstormed ideas, Ellie said, "I keep picturing that little girl my parents sponsored...."

"...through World Vision. Yeah, you've mentioned that once or twice over the years. But I feel the same way. It's gonna be even more exciting to actually participate in the mission instead of just sending in money."

Three hours later, Ellie leaned back in her chair. "Do you think that's enough?"

"Oh, I think you need to join a list-makers support group." Cara flipped through a binder that contained the schedule of monthly meetings, fundraising dates, and the donation request list.

Ellie laughed as she opened her duplicate copy. "I'm color-coding mine. Don't mock."

"I'm not, just suggesting you get some help." Cara closed the binder. "Seriously, you are good at all this. You'd be a fantastic event planner."

"I do like it. I'm sure my kids' birthday parties will be epic." What was the point of thinking about a career when all she wanted was to be Dylan's wife and mother of his children?

5

Monday night, Ellie dragged herself home. Cheer practice had been long and the customers at the clothing boutique had been difficult. Her plan to collapse on the couch for some much-needed relaxation evaporated when she found her mom and Dylan's mom sitting at the dining room table with papers spread everywhere.

"Hey, sweet girl." Her mom didn't even look up.

"Hi, Mom, Mrs. Linda." Mrs. Linda's bright lime green top contrasted with her mom's demure black cardigan and pearls. "What are y'all up to?"

The two ladies had gone through a scrapbooking phase, quilting phase, and most recently, an extreme couponing phase. Linda found the great ideas and got excited about them, but her mom followed through with the action.

"We're organizing college applications for you and Dylan. Come sit." Her mom shuffled some papers and handed them to Ellie to see. "Linda, when we were back in college, did you ever think our kids would fall in love and plan to go off to college together?"

"Goodness no! In fact, I never imagined being old enough to have kids going to college." Linda laughed.

"Mom, we've never talked about some of these schools." Ellie's brow wrinkled as she flipped through applications for schools in the Midwest. "Dylan and I have always talked about the East Coast or staying in Texas."

"Dylan said y'all did. These are some he's interested in for football," Linda replied.

"We never talked about these schools. We made a list like a year ago and haven't discussed it since. Of course, we both got applications for Ohio State University, but even though y'all loved it there, I want to be closer to family." Ellie's shoulders slumped. Why would Dylan tell his mom he mentioned these schools when he hadn't?

Her mom arched her eyebrows and patted Ellie's hand. "I'm sure y'all discussed it and you forgot."

Of course Mom would take his side.

"I wouldn't forget changing my college plans." Ellie tossed the papers back on the table. "I guess I'll talk to Dylan."

"I'm sure it's just a misunderstanding, Ellie." Linda stood up and grabbed Ellie in a hug. "You know the plan has always been for you and Dylan to go the same college and get married after graduation. Just like your parents did."

"I know." Ellie pulled away from the hug. *Perhaps it's y'all's dream, but it doesn't seem to be Dylan's dream anymore.*

Maybe a jog would help her get control of her feelings. Before changing her clothes, she sent Dylan a quick text. Your mom's here organizing college apps. Why'd you tell her you had talked to me about these new schools when you didn't?

After pacing ten minutes without a reply, Ellie slipped out through the back door and started her run. Toby Mac's song "Me Without You" played on her iPhone. What would her life be like without Dylan? Sure, all couples went through rough times, especially when they started dating as young as she and Dylan had. But after so many years together, every memory involved him. He was the first boy, the only boy, she had ever loved, and for as long as she could remember, he was the only one who mattered. She ran faster and faster, but her thoughts raced ahead of her until she couldn't catch them.

An hour later she stepped into the shower. The run hadn't helped. Why hadn't Dylan talked to her about applying to those colleges? Did he just assume she would do whatever he wanted? Did he forget? Or, could he see himself without her? The water got hot enough to burn. It washed away the sweat, but it couldn't wash away her fears. For years, her mom and Mrs. Linda had planned her life until she had adopted it as her own dream, never considering a life that didn't involve Dylan.

What would she do if Dylan had a different dream?

The next morning, after a fitful sleep, Ellie found a text from Dylan.

`Those are the colleges sending scouts. No time to talk to you about it yet. Sweet dreams.`

Okay, that made sense. They had always said if Dylan could get a football scholarship and Ellie a cheerleading one, they would save a ton of money. Having accountants for fathers, both had savings from the moment their parents saw the two blue lines on the pregnancy tests, but that money could pay for a house instead of college if they earned scholarships.

Rolling over to grab her Bible for her morning reading, Ellie flipped to the book of *Ruth*, one of her favorites since it had a little bit of romance in it. She paused when she read Ruth's words to her mother-in-law Naomi. *Where you go, I will go too.* That applied to Dylan. It didn't matter where he went, she would follow because he already had her heart.

Jumping out of bed, she texted, `College scouts? Awesome!` She had worried for nothing.

By the end of the week, everything was falling into place. Cara had been switched into her government class, the homecoming committee had picked a theme, and best of all, Dylan had tucked a sweet note into her locker, apologizing for not talking to her about the colleges.

When game time arrived Friday night, Ellie couldn't stand still. In the bleachers, her mom was armed with a camera while her dad and Nick carried hotdogs and drinks. Waving up to them, Ellie grinned. She was so blessed: parents who loved her and each other, and a brother who was more funny than annoying.

Turning back to the field, she caught Dylan's eye as he warmed up on the sideline. He winked at her and ran with the team to the locker room for the last-minute pep talk from the coach. Ellie jogged to the goalpost with the cheerleaders to get the banner ready for the team to run through. As they waited for their cue, two cheerleaders she usually avoided, Melissa and Lindsey, chatted nearby.

"Did you hear Josh is single again?" Melissa nudged Lindsey.

"No, he's so hot. I wonder why Sydney broke up with him."

What? Josh and Sydney? When did they start dating?

"I heard he dumped her the week before school started. You know he's never been the same funny, outgoing Josh since he ran off that stage and left Ellie standing there." Melissa started hanging up the sign.

"I don't know how she survived that. To be honest, I was hoping she would fade into oblivion after that. I guess it's not right to say I was happy to see her so embarrassed, but I was." Several cheerleaders had warned Ellie that Lindsey gossiped about her, but she wasn't even trying to whisper her disgust for Ellie.

So much for her mom's desire to have her children around good kids by attending a Christian school. All these two were good at was hiding their cattiness with "Christianese."

Pasting on a sugar-sweet smile, Ellie stepped over to the girls, who didn't even have the decency to blush. "The sign's perfect. Need any help?"

"We're fine. Thanks." Melissa and Lindsey became very busy straightening the sign. Shrugging, Ellie tightened her ponytail and waited for Emma's signal. The first game of the season was about to begin.

To celebrate the win, the gang headed to a bistro with a large outdoor patio. Sitting with their friends, Dylan folded his arm around her shoulder as the guys went over each play and how impressed the scout seemed with their dominance. They laughed and joked until the manager ran them out at closing time.

The ride home was peaceful. Ellie gazed out of the window, listening to the radio and holding Dylan's strong hand. With a little over an hour until curfew, he pulled up to their favorite park, now deserted. After countless games, they had come to this spot to lie back on the hood of his car and pretend to see stars in the city's sky.

Instead of getting out of the car, Dylan held her arm and leaned in to kiss her. She returned the kiss, running her fingers through his hair as he moved closer. Breaking away, Ellie whispered, "I could kiss you like that for the rest of my life."

"Me too, babe." Dylan lowered the back of his seat until he was almost flat. He pulled her on top of him and kissed her again, more passionately. His kisses had held such urgency only one other time — the night before she left, when he wanted more than she was willing to give. As his hands moved under her shirt to caress her back, Ellie answered his fervor with her own.

"Are you finally ready?" Dylan grinned as he started unbuttoning her shirt.

Ellie's eyes snapped open. She pulled away and sank down in her own seat. "No, Dylan, you know how I feel about sex. I thought you felt the same way." She ran her fingers across her lips, raw from his kisses.

"Ellie, we've been together since eighth grade. I've waited a long time." Dylan straightened his seat and rubbed his jaw as he looked at her. "I love you. We know we're getting married one day, so what's the problem?" His eyes pleaded with her. He loved her, and she loved him. They would get married after college.

Married. She'd promised to wait, the same promise Dylan had made when they were fourteen years old during a True Love Waits campaign at church. "The problem is the Bible says it's wrong."

Were they really having this conversation again? The promise ceremony had been beautiful. The glow of lit candles and the pastor's quivering voice as he prayed for them. She and Dylan had even joked that staying pure would be easy since they knew they would marry each other. Sure, guys had sex on the brain most of the day, but Dylan was committed to making the right choice as she was. Or at least he had been.

"Do you think God cares if we have sex now or in five years when we're married? We love each other and are committed to each other. Why would a piece of paper matter when our hearts are already there?" The car got hotter and hotter until she finally had to get out. Moving onto the grass, she took a few steps, letting the breeze cool her. When she turned back to the car, Dylan was standing by the door, his eyes stormy.

"Yes, I think God cares. Don't you?" Ellie strode toward him and reached out to touch his arms, but he sidestepped her.

"I think you're so concerned about following rules and doing what other people tell you is the right thing to do that you don't enjoy life. Who cares what they say?" Dylan slammed his hand on the hood of the car.

"I don't care what they think, but I care what God thinks." Ellie inched away from his anger. "I thought you felt the same way."

"Well, I don't, Ellie, and waiting for you is getting old. You wouldn't believe what the guys tell me in the locker room." He leaned back against the car and crossed his arms.

Ellie cut him off. "Didn't you just say we shouldn't care what other people say?"

"I don't care. I'm just saying we're the only ones just kissing." Dylan ran his fingers through his hair and opened her door. "Just get in. Let's go home."

"Don't you want to talk about it?" Ellie froze. He walked around to his side of the car as if nothing had happened. *Why am I having to beg him to work things out?*

"What's there to talk about? We disagree, and there's nothing I can do to change your mind." Dylan turned the car on and waited for her to get in.

"Don't be mad, Dylan. You know I love you." Ellie buckled her seat belt as he peeled out of the parking lot.

"I know, Ellie. Just not enough."

"Or maybe you don't love me enough. True love waits." Ellie muttered as she stared out of the window. They weren't going to get past this argument any time soon. The silence weighed heavily, and Ellie jumped out of the car before Dylan could get out to open the door for her. As she slammed the door to make her point, he didn't even move to walk her to the door. Instead, he put the car in reverse and fled without a second glance.

Ellie texted Cara as she walked into the house. Her best friend's ability to talk for hours without coming up for air would be the perfect distraction. Engrossed in a movie, her parents barely glanced up when she asked for permission to spend the night at Cara's house. Thankfully, Cara immediately replied that she would have ice cream and a movie ready.

Driving to Cara's, Ellie cranked up the music and rolled down the window, letting the wind dry her tears. She took slow, deep breaths of the refreshing night air. Why was doing the right thing so hard? Although Dylan's arguments made sense, the memory of her 13th birthday dinner roared through her head. She had had a party with her friends, but her dad had asked her if she would go to a special dinner with him that night.

Dressed in a business suit, he showed up at the front door of their house with flowers and drove her to a fancy restaurant in the heart of Houston. After dinner, they asked for dessert to go and shared it on the family swing in their backyard. Her dad talked about how a godly man treats a woman he loves, putting the woman's needs first.

Her dad shared details about his first date with Ellie's mother. Trying to impress his future wife, he had taken her to a fancy restaurant where he hadn't been able to pronounce anything on the menu and ended up ordering squid. They had laughed about it the rest of the evening, and he knew it was the reason he had gotten a second date.

Then his tone became serious. "Ellie, I loved your mom from the moment I saw her. She was determined not to be like your grandmother, so she played hard to get, but our life together now was worth the wait. And I'm so glad we waited until we were married to have sex."

Ellie cringed. "Dad, I've heard the sex talk before. I know to wait. Let's talk about something else."

"Let me at least pray for you." His sincere words asking God to keep her heart pure and full of love for Jesus before she loved others clothed Ellie with security and a strength that she could follow God's perfect will. She had echoed her dad's prayer in her heart, vowing to do the right thing to please Him.

In all the years she and Dylan had been together, Dylan had always treated her the way her dad had that night. Like a princess. But something changed when they had argued right before she left for the summer, and there was nothing she could do if he refused to talk about it. In both instances, she had chosen the best, not because her parents told her what was right but because she had made a promise to Jesus on the night of her birthday and again during her church's ceremony the next year. *I can't believe I almost let Dylan talk me into it.*

As she approached Cara's street, she rolled up the windows and put back on her happy face. Used to hiding behind a smile, she'd have to give an Oscar-worthy performance to pull off disguising her emotions tonight.

Ringing the doorbell, Ellie took a step back when Josh answered the door. Since the fiasco at the play, he avoided the house when she was over. Maybe the short notice threw him off.

His dark hair was wet, and his shirt was stretched over his broad shoulders. Most girls at her school would do anything to go out with Josh. Despite his popularity, he seemed to prefer quiet get-togethers with a small crowd over single dates or big parties. Maybe that explained why he was at home before midnight on a Friday night.

"Is Cara home?" Even though it was a silly question, there wasn't much else to say. She stared at the ground, so he couldn't see her puffy, red eyes.

"Yeah, she's in her room." Josh stepped aside and let her in.

"Thanks. Congrats on the win tonight. You played well. Two touchdowns." *Why am I standing here rambling like an idiot?*

After locking the door, Josh pivoted around to face her again. He finally looked into her eyes, and Ellie didn't bother trying to avoid his stare. Josh had the ability to see past her pretenses anyway.

"You deserve someone better, Lansing." He spoke so quietly, Ellie strained to catch each word.

"What?" Ellie tilted her head and pursed her lips.

"You heard me. You deserve better than a guy who's going to make you cry. You deserve the best." Josh's voice was still barely above a whisper as he passed her in the hall.

He was gone before she had a good retort. How dare he tell her what she deserved or didn't deserve after his nonperformance at the play. Like everyone else, did he expect perky little Ellie to keep smiling no matter what?

"Talking to yourself? They have counselors for that." Cara joked as she waved Ellie to her room.

"It's only bad when you hear yourself answer back. Or is that about the voices in your head." Ellie tried to laugh but could only tear up as they sat on Cara's bed. In between bites of ice cream, Ellie poured out the story. "It sounds just as bad telling it out loud as it was being there."

"What a jerk! I don't even know what to say." Cara's voice got louder and a little higher with every word.

"Quiet, I don't want your parents to hear." Mrs. Martin would probably want to call Dylan's parents.

"The whole world should hear he's a loser who expects his girlfriend to do whatever he wants." Cara had never had a boyfriend, so she couldn't understand. Everything was black and white to Cara. Either Dylan was the one, or he wasn't. He was a good guy or a jerk. There were no shades of gray.

Ellie blew out the breath she'd been holding. "He's not a jerk. I know he loves me, but you know how guys are. Didn't you just tell me the other day that we're the perfect couple?"

Cara winced and shook her head. "I shouldn't have said that, Ellie. No one's perfect, and I know you feel you're supposed to have it all together. But, you're a mere mortal like the rest of us."

"It's okay. You would think after years of trying to live up to my mom's expectations, I wouldn't go around calling what Dylan and I have the perfect relationship. It sets up disappointment. I just don't get guys. They all sat through the same group discussions in Sunday school that we did, so why don't they have the same standards as us?" Ellie shoved a way-too-big spoonful of ice cream into her mouth, tensing for the coming brain freeze.

"Yeah, they're always thinking about one thing. This is why I don't date. Why waste my time until I'm ready to get hitched?" Cara pointed her spoon at Ellie.

"I can't wait to see you in love, Cara. I should record all this to play back for you when you start gushing about how hot some guy is." Ellie pulled out her phone to pretend to record Cara. Instead, she checked her messages. Nothing from Dylan. Couldn't he even say he was sorry for hurting her?

For years, Ellie had watched girls cry in the school bathroom about some guy treating them like garbage, or sleeping with them and dumping them, or not calling them back after a first date. And now she was one of those girls, crying into a bowl of ice cream on a Friday night because her boyfriend hadn't texted. *I shouldn't have judged those girls; I should have handed them a tissue and chocolate.*

"I thought you might want to watch a comedy." Cara pulled Ellie's phone out of her hand.

"Let's watch *The Princess Bride*." Although most teens her age had never even heard of the movie, Ellie's mom had forced her to watch it so many times that it was now one of her go-to movies for just about any occasion.

"As you wish." Cara laughed at one of the movie's one-liners. "Let me clean up the ice cream, and you can get it going."

On the way to the den, there was a light in Mrs. Martin's craft room, where she made bows and monogrammed children's clothes that she sold online. Ellie popped her head in. Unlike her own all-too-perfect mom, Cara's mom was casual and down-to-earth. She wore her mismatched clothes with confidence, rarely wore make-up, and had never lost the pregnancy weight from the twins, but she loved people as no one else did. She was one of Ellie's favorite adults. Mrs. Martin would wrap her arms around her and say a prayer of comfort without even asking if she was okay.

Instead of Mrs. Martin, Josh was in the craft room. His back to her, head nodding to the music pumping through his headphones, he brushed bold strokes of paint across a canvas. Ellie took a moment to watch him work. He'd always doodled in classes, but obviously his talent went much deeper.

He was transferring a scene from a sketch to canvas. In vivid oranges and blue, he created a rocky beach at sunset. The scene took her to Nantucket beach again, watching the waves and getting a glimpse of how big God is.

He spun around and blocked her view of his work. "What's up?" He took off his headphones, and his brown eyes showed the same compassion he had shown her earlier that evening.

"Sor-sorry." Ellie stuttered. "I thought your mom would be in here, and then I got distracted by your painting."

"Well, she went to bed." Josh started to turn back to his painting, obviously expecting her to leave.

"It's beautiful, Josh." He turned again. He said nothing, so she continued. "It reminds me of my summer in Nantucket. You captured it perfectly, almost like you were there."

"Maybe one day." Josh stepped to the side so that she could see the painting in its entirety. Sitting on one of the rocks was a girl facing the ocean with her long curly blonde hair drifting in the breeze. "Ellie, there's something—"

"Ellie, are you coming?" Cara's voice interrupted whatever Josh was going to say. "J, that's amazing." Cara put her hand on her brother's shoulder as she inspected the painting. "This may be one of the best you've done. Don't you love it, Ellie?"

"It's breathtaking." Ellie couldn't tear her gaze from the painting. It was as if God was reminding her, as He had done that summer, that the God in control of the whole universe was big enough to handle her life too. *Thank you, God.*

"We're going to watch *The Princess Bride* if you want to join us later."

Cara must have forgotten that Josh never hung out with them anymore. Or maybe she was helping God answer her prayer for them all to be friends again.

"Nah, I've reached my torture limit with that movie. Besides, I want to finish this while it's fresh in my mind." Putting his headphones on, Josh shut himself off from more conversation.

As they set up the movie, Ellie poked Cara. "When did Josh start painting?"

"This summer. After the fight with Dylan, he quit hanging out with most of the guys and started painting from the drawings he had done before. He hasn't really shown me any of his work. You know how private he can be about his feelings." Cara pressed play on the remote, and the girls lost themselves in the movie, falling asleep on the couches before the ending credits.

Ellie jerked awake, shaking and out of breath. It was three in the morning. She had been dreaming about the peaceful Nantucket Bay, much like the scene Josh had painted. Then suddenly, the waves had begun crashing over the rocks where she was sitting. Although she tried climbing back to the safety of the road, the waves grew bigger and lapped her legs, pulling her into their swell. As she struggled against the force of the sea, she grew exhausted and woke up as she let the waves overtake her.

Ellie slowed her breathing to match Cara's rhythm. But what did the dream mean? Was it stress about Dylan, or was it a sign of what was to come?

6

By Sunday afternoon, Dylan still hadn't called. He had planned to go to Texas A&M with some of the football team to watch the game on Saturday. Maybe he had come home late that night and skipped church in the morning.

But when Dylan didn't show up for youth group Sunday night, Ellie asked his mom where he was.

"He said he was behind on school work from the busy weekend, so he stayed home."

He had to be avoiding her. Even though he should be the one to apologize, she sent him a text. `I hope you had fun at the game. Miss you.` Bringing up the fight would just lead to another one.

Her phone chimed. `Game was good. Miss you too. See you tomorrow.` Another text came through. `A&M would be an awesome choice for college. What do you think?`

Ellie had to smile. He was including her in college plans!

`Gig 'em. <3` She replied, sending him the university's slogan, followed by a heart.

Ellie woke up early Monday morning. She made mental notes about her classes, cheer practice, and the mission trip meeting. Taking a quick shower, she settled on her beanbag in front of her bedroom mirror to straighten her hair.

As the flat iron worked its magic, she planned the coming days. Homecoming was only three weeks away and, like the rest of her life, she wanted it to be perfect. Although Waltham was more of a college prep than a religious Christian private school, the administration had strict rules on dances and parties. Themes had to "encourage group fun," but since most of the students had grown up together, they didn't mind. One of the first graduating classes had started a tradition of a costume party for homecoming, saving the formal wear for prom. This year's theme was the 1950s. Ellie had found a pink poodle skirt that would twirl in a big circle when Dylan spun her around.

Members of the homecoming court since freshman year, surely Ellie and Dylan would be named once again. The fairy tale would be perfect as she was crowned queen with Dylan by her side as king.

"Hey, Ellie girl." Her dad knocked on her doorframe and stepped just inside. "You're up early."

"Just straightening my hair."

Her dad sat next to her on the floor and gave her hair a shake. "I remember when you were a little baby with those blonde curls. Your mom swore she would never cut it because it was so beautiful."

"I guess a modern-day Rapunzel would be cool." They laughed at the image.

"Well, I've always liked it curly." His tone became serious. "I don't know why you waste so much time straightening out the beauty God gave you."

"You know Dylan loves it straight. And I'm not really in the mood for a lecture about true beauty today." She turned back to the mirror.

"Ellie, your selflessness is one of the things I love most about you. You try to make everyone around you happy, and while I think it's Christ-like to love others as yourself, I don't think Jesus requires that you be someone other than what He created you to be."

"It's just hair. Don't make a big deal about it." Ellie wrinkled her nose. Her dad was usually more laid back and low key than this. Why was he being so serious?

"I know you think it's just hair, but your mom told me about the college applications. I want you to follow your own dreams, not someone else's. Don't lose yourself in your efforts to please Dylan." He took her hand and put the straightener down. "I was hoping you'd see that during your summer away."

"I love Dylan, and a couple months apart didn't change that. I've loved him since before I knew what love was. When I just wanted to be around him all the time and didn't know why." Ellie watched her dad in the mirror. His face held new wrinkles, and his hair was getting grayer by the day.

"I know you do, Eleanor, but since you came back from Nantucket, I can see a difference. You seem anxious, and I know you don't want to talk about some things with me. But, I want you to know I woke up earlier than usual this morning with a deep burden to pray for you, for your resolve to follow Jesus first." His eyes, the same dark brown as her own, welled up with concern. He cupped her face and smiled.

Ellie couldn't hide anything from her dad. He could always see through the happy face her mother fell for. "Senior year is hard. So many changes, and you know I don't do change."

She pulled a long curl down, released it and it bounced back up.

"You know God knows the plans He has for your future. Even if they don't turn out the way you planned, they're great plans. You're a special girl, strong in your faith like not many teenagers are. Can I say a prayer over you before you finish your straightening transformation?"

"You bet." Ellie put her hands in her dad's strong hands. His words washed over her spirit just like when she was little and he had prayed with her every night before bed. While his words today whispered for her to be who God wanted her to be and for Him to give her strength in the days to come, Ellie's silent prayer was for everything with Dylan to work out. Surely God would bless her with a great life. After all, she followed all of the rules and guidelines her parents and youth leaders said Christians should do. Didn't God owe her a reward for her obedience?

A note was taped to her locker. *Meet me at our spot for lunch. Can't wait to see you.* The tree in the courtyard was just right for sneaking away for a few minutes of alone time. Every once in a while, they had lunch there when their schedules were too hectic for longer dates.

When lunch arrived, Ellie darted out to their spot to wait for Dylan, but he had gotten there first. He had his jacket spread out for her to sit on, and a lunch from off campus awaited her. "You're the best." Ellie greeted him with a long kiss before sitting down and taking a drink of lemonade.

"I do my best." Dylan dug into his food but didn't take his gaze off her. "I know you want to talk about our fight."

"Nope, I don't. I just want to enjoy this perfect moment. The food is amazing, and I'm ready to snuggle with my hot man." After they ate in silence, Ellie picked up their trash and leaned back against his muscular chest. His touch was tender as he played with her hair. All too soon, the bell sounded. Stealing a quick kiss, they promised to call each other later that night.

Almost half the class showed up to volunteer at the mission trip meeting after school. Ellie handed out assignments, and the room buzzed with conversation as groups bounced around ideas. Ellie walked around the room, answering questions and making notes. This trip was going to be epic.

A night of catching up on recorded TV shows would be the perfect ending to a great day. Ellie threw down her backpack.

Her parents were sitting on the couch, holding hands and cuddling like she and Dylan had done just a few hours before.

"Come into the den, sweet girl. Nicholas, come down, son." Her dad shouted toward the stairs.

Why is Dad home so early?

When Nick clomped down the stairs, his expression was full of confusion, confirming that something was up.

"Ellie, Nick, we have some bad news. There's no easy way to say it." Her dad's voice shook.

"Just spit it out, Dad," Nicholas advised. Ellie nodded.

Her mom said, "I noticed a lump in my last self-exam, so I went to the doctor."

Ellie's heart dropped to her feet. What was coming was not good.

"We got the results today. I have breast cancer."

Tears streamed down her parents' faces as Nick and Ellie joined their parents on the couch.

"God's in control." Her dad's voice was strong despite his tears. "The doctors caught it early, and the prognosis is good."

"I'm going to be okay." Ellie's mom's voice cracked despite her confident words. "I'll have surgery next week to remove the tumor, and then I'll do radiation and a few rounds of chemotherapy after I recover from the surgery."

Ellie was nearly blinded by tears, but her mom was doing what she did best, putting on a smile no matter what she was feeling. She gave her mom a hug. "You're so strong. Amazingly strong. I love you."

"I love you too, Eleanor." Ellie crinkled her nose at her full name. "You know we named you after my grandmother, but I'm thinking of another Eleanor, the former first lady. I believe she said it best, 'A woman is like a tea bag; you can't tell how strong she is until you put her in hot water.' We're going to get through this as a family." She wiped away Ellie's tears and turned to Nicholas, who was staring at the wall.

Embracing him in a hug, she whispered in his ear, which only made him cry harder. Ellie faced her dad. "Is this why you prayed for God to give me strength this morning?"

"Yes, I knew we had the doctor's appointment today and might get bad news." He glanced over at her mom with a look of love usually seen only in movies and cleared his throat, gaining his composure. "This is going to try all of us, and I knew I would need your help to get the family through this. I also know you love Dylan, but I felt the Lord was telling me you need to find your own way, not just follow Dylan's path."

Ellie grabbed her dad's hand and leaned against his chest, watching her mom. As the four of them shed their last tears for the night, Ellie's dad led the family in a prayer for health, strength, and God's will to be done.

7

After a few hours of restless sleep, Ellie struggled to get out of bed the next morning. When she opened her door, she found a note. *Go back to sleep. I'll take you to school late. Love, Mom.* She fell back into her comfy bed, but couldn't get back to sleep. *Cancer.* Ellie had participated in an awareness fundraising run with the cheerleaders last year and donated twenty bucks when a group on campus was raising money, but cancer had always been something that happened to other families, not hers.

Sitting up, she pulled out her iPad and looked up breast cancer. Her mom's tumor was stage one, which meant the doctors had caught it early, promising a good chance of full remission. Still, Ellie's hands started shaking as she read about cancer, treatment, and all the horrible side effects. This was supposed to be the best year of her life, and now she would spend it caring for her mom, who could even die. The whole situation just sucked. Ellie grimaced. *Get over yourself. Mom may die, and you're worried about your social life.*

Staring at the ceiling fan, imagining every possible scenario, Ellie had to do something. Jumping up, she searched her closet for a journal she had made in 10th grade. The youth group had been studying scriptures that applied to real-life feelings: anger, lust, fear, failure, etc. Although most of her youth group had participated in the discussion, they had all teased Ellie for going overboard. She had written the scriptures into a journal each week, along with notes from the youth pastor's lessons. She flipped through the journal until the title of the page read "Scriptures for when you feel scared."

Ellie read them aloud. While they all spoke life, one stood out because it was Jesus talking in John 14:27. "Peace I leave with you; my peace I give you. I do not give to you as the world gives. Do not let your hearts be troubled and do not be afraid." Ellie repeated the words until they were etched in her brain. She fell asleep clutching the words of truth.

Two hours later, she awakened to her mom sitting on the edge of the bed, reading the journal. "I didn't mean to read your private journal, but it was open, and I couldn't help notice it was scriptures. I hope you don't mind."

"No, of course not." Ellie sat up and rubbed her eyes. Her mom appeared the same as she always had. Khaki capris, a button-down flowered shirt with a pink cardigan. Her low heels and French twist completed the pulled-together look. She didn't seem sick. Maybe the doctors had made a mistake.

"These scriptures were just what I needed. I couldn't sleep, worried that you kids would be stressed or nervous about what's coming up. Seeing this brings me joy. Your dad and I have prayed since you were a little girl that you would trust in Him, and to know you looked to Him when you got bad news gives me strength to make it through this." Ellie's mom leaned over and kissed Ellie on the forehead. "Get dressed. I'm going to wake Nick up and then take you both to school."

Climbing out of bed, Ellie checked her phone. She had one message—from Cara. Where are you?

Before getting into the shower, she replied. Will be there in a bit. Need to talk to you. How was she supposed to tell people her mom had cancer when she didn't want to believe it herself? And why hadn't Dylan texted? Had her mom told Mrs. Linda, who then told Dylan, or did they want Ellie to tell him? No sense worrying about it. There were bigger things to think about now.

After checking in late while her mom gave the news to the school counselor, Ellie raced down the hall. Lunch was the perfect time to catch up with Dylan and Cara. Finding her best friend in the hall, she pulled her into the nearest bathroom and spilled everything, from the bad news to the strength she had found in scripture that morning. Cara wrapped her arms around Ellie and cried with her. Touching up their smudged mascara, Ellie said, "Cara, you're more than a friend. You're a sister. What would I do without you?"

"I hope we never have to find out because there's a chance you would walk around with raccoon eyes." They shared a laugh, breaking the moment as two girls ambled in.

With one last hug, Ellie left to find Dylan, who was probably with his teammates. Texting him as she rounded the corner, Ellie plowed into someone.

"They say texting and walking can be just as dangerous as texting and driving." Josh was bending over to pick up the notebooks she had knocked out of his hands.

"I'm so sorry, Josh. Let me help you." Ellie reached down to pick up a notebook that had fallen open to a full-page sketch. The same beach scene as the one in his painting, but this time, the girl was sitting on a surfboard riding a big wave. But the girl wasn't surfing. She was merely sitting as she had been in the painting before, as if she was oblivious to the wave and its size.

"This picture goes with the painting. Is it the same girl?" *Argh, I should've kept my mouth shut. I don't want Josh thinking I care about the girl he was drawing.* And maybe it's not even the same girl since it only shows her back and long curly hair.

"Yeah, it's the same girl. This is the second time I've seen you crying in the last week, Lansing. What's up?" Although they wouldn't quite meet hers, Josh's eyes showed concern.

"Life. I'm sure Cara will fill you in. I don't have time to talk. I need to find Dylan. But…. it's nice of you to ask." Ellie fiddled with the buttons on her uniform sweater. There was so much resentment in their past, but with her mom's news, not much else mattered — even Josh's mistake. "See you later."

"You too." Josh didn't move as Ellie rushed past him and down the hall to Dylan, who was waiting with open arms.

"My mom told me the news this morning. I'm so sorry." Dylan's arms were strong and secure. But why hadn't he called or texted when he found out? "I wanted to call you, but Mom said you were sleeping in and would be at school later."

Ellie's heartbeat slowed. *Why am I being so sensitive, analyzing his every comment like it's an English class discussing Shakespeare?*

"I'm okay now that you're holding me. I'm so scared, Dylan." Tears swam in her eyes.

"Your mom is tougher than you know. She's going to be fine. And I'm here if you need me." Dylan whispered against her hair.

"I do. Please don't let go." And for the next ten minutes, he didn't.

The rest of the week passed in a blur. Ellie went through the motions of her routine like a zombie. Instead of hanging out with friends, she rushed home to help her mom give the entire house a deep cleaning even though her mom never let a speck of dust land in her house, cook and freeze meals for after the surgery, and just be together.

Although her mom never admitted she was nervous, the house had been completely cleaned every day from the baseboards to the ceiling fans. Ellie's dad joked it was spring-cleaning on steroids. Her dad and Nick stuck close to home too, and the family laughed as they got the house in order for when their "director," as her dad loved to call her mom, would be out of commission for a few weeks of recovery.

Cara and the cheer squad had been amazing, praying for her mom at practice and sending Ellie encouraging texts and emails. Her boss had been understanding about her skipping work, and her teachers gave her the next few assignments early so that she wouldn't fall behind.

The only person missing was Dylan. Since their sweet moment in the hallway, he seemed distant when they talked, as if he wasn't sure what to say or do. When she called him out on it, he replied that she had been the one pulling away, too busy to hang out that week. Slumping into the chair that sat next to her bedroom window, she ended the conversation with *I love you* and hung up.

The true mystery was the scripture drop, as she and Cara dubbed it. Each morning and sometimes during the day, Ellie opened her locker to find a scripture written on an index card. The handwriting, bold strokes and all caps, was vaguely familiar.

At the end of the week, Ellie brought the cards home, putting her favorites around her room. As she continued to read in her old journal, she compared her list to the cards. They were the same. Since almost half of the senior class was involved in her church youth group, it could be anyone. Whoever it was, Ellie made up excuses to check her locker for more.

The football team won again on Friday night. Then the whole family holed up in the house to spend time together for the rest of the weekend. Finally, surgery day arrived. The Lansing family was ready to kick cancer's butt. Their pastors joined them at the hospital to pray before the surgery, and Ellie tipped her head back, closing her eyes in the peace for just a minute. Her parents knew she and Nick wouldn't be able to focus on school, so they agreed to let them come to the hospital.

The surgery went on longer than expected. Nick paced, her dad tried to work on his laptop, and Ellie twisted her senior ring around, watching it glimmer in the sun's rays. Waiting was like riding a wave of emotions, the calm and then the rocky wave. Like the drawing in Josh's sketch pad. He had perfectly captured her turmoil even though he hadn't known about her mom's cancer when he drew it. Just when she'd rubbed her finger raw from twirling her ring, the doctor came out. The trio jumped up to meet him, joining hands without even noticing.

"We are confident we got the entire tumor. It was a little larger than we expected, but the margins were clear, and the surgery went well. We also inserted the port for her chemo treatments while she was sedated." The doctor smiled and shook her dad's hand.

Ellie and Nick fell into their dad's embrace. He thanked the doctor. "Praise God! When can we see her?"

"She'll be in recovery for a bit, and then we'll assign her a room. A nurse will be here shortly to give you more information." The doctor left.

"Let me call your grandparents and Pastor Mark first, and then you guys can let your friends know." Five years of stress had melted off his face as compared to two hours ago.

"I can't wait to tell Dylan." Ellie called as soon as she got the thumbs up from her dad. Nick was searching through his contact list to make a group text. Dylan's phone rang. And rang. *Why isn't he picking up?* School was out for the day, and he had promised to keep his phone nearby during practice.

Ellie hung up and called Cara instead. Cara answered on the first ring and offered to skip cheer to come by. She told Ellie she had checked her locker and was bringing a few notes that had been dropped in.

"No, stay. I just wanted to let you know. I'll call you later." Ending the call, Ellie sighed. *At least I have one friend who keeps her word.*

She got Dylan's voicemail for the second time and left a brief message as the nurse called them to her mom's room. Ellie's heart pounded as they entered. *Have I ever seen her without make-up and a coordinated outfit? How will she look in a hospital bed?*

Her mom smiled and reached her hand toward her family. "How'd it go?"

"It went great, baby. They got the entire tumor." Ellie's dad brushed back her mom's hair. He laid a gentle kiss on her forehead.

"As long as I have y'all, I'm fine no matter what." Her eyes drifted open and shut as if staying awake was a struggle. "Just don't let anyone see me like this." *Yep, she's the same old Mom.* Ellie sent a text telling her friends not to come to the hospital.

"Go to sleep, my love. I'll be here when you wake up." Ellie's dad tucked the covers around her mom. He took her hand as he sat in the chair next to the hospital bed. Ellie smiled at the picture of love in front of her. Once when Ellie had come down with the flu, Dylan had brought her some chicken noodle soup, but he just dropped it off. She had joked that he wasn't a very good nurse. How would Dylan treat her if she got really sick?

"You two go home and sleep there tonight, Ellie."

"You need sleep too. Come home with us."

"In our twenty years of marriage, your mom and I have only spent the night apart a few times, and tonight won't be one of them."

"Then we can stay here, Dad. I don't want to leave you." Ellie watched her hero, a man who loved his wife and kids second only to Jesus.

"I'm not alone. I've got my best girl here, and she's asleep, which means I'll finally have her all to myself without her talking." He grinned.

"Call me when she wakes up. I'll keep my ringer turned up loud." Ellie gave her dad a hug. "I hope Dylan is like you when we get married."

"I don't know who you'll marry, but I pray he loves you like I love your mom." Ellie's dad gave Nick a hug, and Ellie leaned over to give her mom one last kiss on the cheek.

"Come on, Nick, let's leave the lovebirds alone." Her earlier coffee worn off, Ellie struggled to keep her eyes open on the way home. She cranked up the music and rolled down the windows, which helped. Once home, she texted Cara and Dylan, letting them know her mom was fine. After setting the alarm and making sure Nick was settled in his room, Ellie fell asleep on her bed without even changing her clothes.

9

The next morning was a whirlwind of transporting Nick to school, calling people to update them on her mom, and then finally getting her mom home from the hospital. Just the drive home wore her out enough to crash as soon as she sat down in the recliner, too tired to see the banner the cheerleaders had made or flowers people had sent.

Finally, Friday morning dawned. Homecoming. The big game tonight and the dance tomorrow. But now homecoming didn't seem as a big a deal as it had just a few short weeks before.

At school all day, the buzz was who would be named to the court and who would win queen. Several friends assured Ellie that she and Dylan would be crowned queen and king. Putting on a fake smile, Ellie joined the conversation, joking about past dance fun and the weekend's events. Between forced laughs, Ellie counted down the hours until she could get home.

By the time the game rolled around, butterflies awakened in her stomach just like the last three homecoming games. *So much for saying I don't care about making the court.* She touched up her make-up in the girls' locker room. She and Dylan hadn't had much time together this week. Although he had come over one night with his mom, he hadn't asked to hang out other than that. His visit had been a little awkward, sitting on the couch while their moms planned their homecoming date as if they weren't there. At least he texted to say he was giving her time with her family and would catch up with her at school. But other than pre-calculus, she hadn't seen him.

Ellie ran onto the field with the other cheerleaders, the wind blowing through her ponytail, lifting her mood as well as her hair. Flipping in handsprings across the field to the crowd's cheers, her adrenaline pumped with each turn. Lining up with the squad, Ellie waved and greeted the fans, scanning the crowd for her dad, who planned to come if he felt her mom was okay at home. A friend from church promised to stay with Ellie's mom so that her dad and Nick could watch Ellie perform. There he was, camera in hand, ready to record her last homecoming game. Blowing him a kiss, Ellie turned to the squad captain for instructions.

The first half flew by as the Waltham Eagles scored three touchdowns and took a commanding 21-7 lead into halftime. Dylan was on fire tonight, throwing three touchdown passes to Josh. As Dylan called out the plays to the offensive line, Ellie imagined him playing college ball and her cheering on the sidelines, perhaps in a uniform too.

The cheerleaders performed a peppy dance routine to a Skillet song, entertaining the crowd as the parents set up the field for the presentation of the homecoming court. Sprinting off the field, Ellie searched the sea of players for Dylan and found him talking to his dad on the sideline. She gave him a wave, but he never looked her way.

He's always super focused during a game. Quit bothering him. Ellie focused her attention on the announcer, who was already calling the sophomore princess. Squeals exploded from the squad as Vanessa's name was called, and Ellie joined in the praise for her little cheer sister. The junior princess was someone Ellie didn't know, and then it was time for the seniors. Ellie crossed her fingers and glanced back at Dylan, who had finally finished talking to his dad. He gave her a weak smile and a slow wink. He always laughed at her excitement over this sort of thing, and because they had both been on the court since freshman year, he often told her they should let someone else win.

As the PTO president started to announce the winners of the court, she paused. "Well, this is a little different than what I expected."

Ellie wrinkled her brow and forced her legs to steady. For someone who two hours ago thought this didn't matter, she sure was anxious to hear the results.

"Our homecoming queen is the lovely and graceful Eleanor Lansing." Applause thundered, and Ellie was surrounded in a group hug of blue and white cheer uniforms. Breaking away from the huddle, she rushed to the field and took the flowers as the principal placed a crown on her head. She searched the bleachers for her dad and smiled her best grin. Her mom would expect myriad pictures for her next scrapbook project. Dylan was still on the sidelines, standing with his dad, but now his gaze was fixed on her. Ellie let a single tear slip down her face. She was so blessed. Her mom's surgery had gone well. Her classmates had chosen her, and Dylan's look of love captivated her.

"Escorting Ellie and serving as homecoming king is Mr. Joshua Martin."

What?!

Ellie forced a smile on her face as Josh stood next to her, his elbow extended for her as they placed the crown on his head.

"Well deserved, Lansing." His smile was for the crowd but his words for her. "You're definitely a queen."

"I don't know about that. I just hope you won't bail on me this time and embarrass me in front of everyone again." Ellie focused on Dylan, who was standing on the sidelines, as Josh guided her down the field.

"I never meant to hurt you. I wanted to explain what happened." His voice was thick with emotion.

"You never once tried to tell me anything, Josh. That's what hurt the most. It was one of the worst nights in my life, and it wasn't even important enough to you to say you were sorry." Her jaw was beginning to hurt from clenching her teeth while still smiling. The football field stretched longer with each step.

"What are you talking about? I tried to apologize, but you didn't show up." Josh turned to face her as they reached the end of the field.

"What?" Ellie looked up into his soft brown eyes that shone in the darkening sky.

"Yeah, I—" Josh's eyes clouded over.

"Thanks for walking with my girl, Martin. I've got it from here." Dylan took Ellie's hand and cupped her face with his hands, bringing his lips down to meet hers. Ellie stood on her tiptoes and brought her arms around his neck as if holding on to a life preserver. After the last two weeks of turmoil, this moment was perfect. Finally, he pulled away, gave her a quick peck on the forehead, and wrapped his arm around her to pose for the cameras.

"Even if you didn't win, you're still my king." Ellie's cheeks were aching. She gazed up at Dylan's face, and her smile faltered. *That's a fake smile. What's going on?* She followed his gaze. A girl she had never seen before, sitting alone on the edge of the bleachers. Short dark hair and brooding eyes made a striking contrast to her pale skin, and she was staring back at Dylan. *Who is that? And why is my boyfriend staring at her?*

As she drew a breath, the coach called the team back to the field to prepare for the second half. Dylan and Josh ran to the huddle, leaving Ellie to walk back to the cheerleaders alone.

The rest of the game was a frenzy of touchdowns. The Eagles clobbered the Cougars, 49-7. The team ran off the field in victory, and Ellie watched the stands as the crowds shuffled out to the parking lot. The strange girl was nowhere to be found. Maybe she was just a Cougars fan who ended up on the wrong side of the field. That wouldn't explain why Dylan was staring at her with such intensity. *You're just paranoid.*

Ellie and Cara showered and changed in the locker room, then walked toward Cara's car. Ellie's parents insisted she spend the night with Cara, wanting Ellie to enjoy the weekend and not to worry about things at home. The Martins had invited the entire football team and the cheerleaders for a party at their house. Unlike most parents, Cara's knew the partying that went on even at a private school, and they often opened up their house to the kids to hang out in a safe environment. Ellie checked her phone. There was a text from her mom.

Congrats. I was on speakerphone with your dad so I could hear the news. I love you and can't wait to see pictures.

Ellie typed a quick reply and faced Cara. "There's something I need to ask you."

"Anything, girl." Cara unlocked the car and they began stuffing their bags into the trunk.

"When we were walking down the field, Josh mentioned that he had tried to apologize to me, but I swear, Cara, he never did. Why'd he make that up?"

"When all that happened, I told you I didn't want to get involved. Josh is my brother, and you're my best friend. It has been so hard to keep my mouth shut. I wish I could lock y'all in a room until you figure it out. But, I promised my mom I wouldn't get in the middle of it, and I'm keeping my word. You'll have to ask Josh. Or Dylan. But that's all I'm saying."

What did Dylan have to do with it? Sending him a quick text, she asked him what time he would be at the party.

His answer came a minute later. I'm not coming. Feeling sick.

What? He had been fine just an hour ago. What could be going on now? And how come every time she needed him lately, he wasn't there?

Ellie stared out of the car window. Cara turned on some music by Lecrae, and Ellie nodded her head to the beat. As they pulled up to Cara's house, Ellie took a deep breath and silently recited scriptures she had read until they were stamped on her heart. As her dad had promised, everything would work together for her good. She would enjoy this night, even if it wasn't going to end with a kiss from Dylan.

10

For an hour, Ellie and her friends laughed and ate more pizza than a girl should consume the night before trying to fit into a costume for homecoming. When the group started dancing, seeing who could be the silliest, Ellie bowed out. She let herself out the back door to sit near the pool. The late September night was still warm, so Ellie let her feet dangle in the water. The cool water reminded her of the barefoot walks she had taken on the beaches of Nantucket. She lay back on the concrete. If only she could see the stars.

"The sky reminds you just how big God is, doesn't it?" Josh was standing nearby but the shadows hid his expression. "I don't want to interrupt your thoughts, Lansing. Can I join you?" He started rolling up his pant legs.

"Well, I guess you already are." She gave a thin smile.

Josh took off his polo shirt. His gray undershirt stretched across his muscles much more than the last time he had been shirtless near her. Her cheeks burned and she averted her eyes.

He folded up his shirt and threw it beside her head. "Put that under your head. The ground's hard."

"I didn't know you cared." As she brought the shirt under her head, his cologne wafted on the breeze. Josh dropped his feet into the water and lay back next to her—close enough to touch.

"You'd be surprised how much I do, Lansing." His voice was quiet. Had she heard him right?

Ellie frowned. "Why do you call me Lansing? I don't know if I've ever asked you that." It would be better to stick to safe topics.

"10th grade. I heard you complaining to Cara that the Spanish teacher made us sit in alphabetical order, so you had Garrett Jacobs in front of you and me behind you. We didn't give you much peace."

"I remember. Y'all made up Spanish words, telling me that was the answer. Then when I would say what you told me, the teacher would think I was trying to be disrespectful." Ellie rolled on her side and pointed her finger at him. "That's the only time I've ever had a teacher call home on me. EVER."

"Be a rebel, Lansing. Every once in a while, it's fun." Josh swatted her hand away. "Anyway, you said you wished your last name wasn't Lansing, so I decided I would remind you every time I talked to you. I'm surprised it took you this long to figure it out. I thought you were labeled gifted."

"If you're going to invade my peaceful moment out here, at least shut up and let me enjoy it." Ellie flopped back and kicked her feet in the water, creating ripples that were a bit like the ocean waves that rushed in and out with the tide.

The lights of downtown Houston colored the sky. They lay in silence until Ellie blurted, "About what you said tonight."

"I thought you wanted silence. But since I'm such a gentleman, what about it?"

"You said you tried to apologize, but I don't remember that." Ellie turned her head to look at him, but his gaze remained on the sky. "I waited months, so I think I would have remembered."

"A few nights before the play, I got a new phone and hadn't added my contacts. So that night, I didn't have your number to call you. You blocked me online, and when I went to your house, your dad said you weren't up to talking to me. Cara refused to get in the middle of it, and Dylan told me you would get over it. I left you a message with Dylan the next day, asking you to meet me at Memorial Park." Josh sat up as he began to talk faster and more passionately. "I waited three hours, and you never showed up."

Ellie sat up, trying to see his face, but he leaned over, looking at the water. "I swear, Josh, I didn't know. Dylan didn't pass on the message."

"Well, he told me you didn't want to be friends anymore and that I should just let it go until you calmed down." Josh took his feet out of the water and faced Ellie. She didn't move as the puddles spread under his wet feet. "I should have tried harder, but I trusted him when he said you would get over it and everything would be back to normal. I should have done more to show you how sorry I was, how that night was my fault."

"Dylan knew how upset I was. I cried for a week at the embarrassment, hearing people gossip, but most of all that you bailed on me. I thought we were friends, and you left me standing on stage alone, looking like an idiot. Then, you couldn't even face me at school or tell me you were sorry." She lifted her feet out of the water and stood. *How could Dylan let me go on and on about what a jerk Josh was not to apologize? And why didn't he give me the message?*

Catching her arm as he stood, Josh tried to face her, but she backed away. "I never meant to hurt you of all people, Lansing. I wish I could go back in time and change it all."

"So, why did you do it? Why did you walk away from me?" Ellie looked him in the eyes.

"Because I was scared." Josh's gaze never left hers.

"Of what?"

"Of you." Josh pushed back the strands of hair that escaped her ponytail. "I don't know why you waste time straightening your hair. It's beautiful curly."

"Stop changing the subject, Josh." Ellie pushed his hand away and stepped back, far enough away that he couldn't touch her. "Tell me why you were scared of me."

"Ellie!" Cara's voice broke the mood as she raced toward them. "Dylan's been in an accident. My dad's going to take us to the hospital."

Ellie stared at Cara. Hadn't Dylan gone home? A car accident? Surely her friend must be mistaken. After a few seconds, Ellie found her voice. "What?"

"Dylan. Hospital. Let's go." Cara grabbed her arm, but Ellie remained frozen. Josh handed Ellie her shoes, and the twins guided her to Mr. Martin's car.

On the way to the hospital, Ellie didn't move, gaping out of the window at the road as it rushed by. Mr. Martin prayed aloud as he drove, asking God to protect Dylan. But something was horribly wrong. Dylan had said he wasn't feeling good, so shouldn't he be at home? So when and how had he been in an accident?

11

Ellie jumped out of the car before it came to a complete stop and ran into the emergency room's lobby. Dylan's parents were huddled together. She raced into their arms. "What happened?"

"He was driving and lost control of the car and drove into a ditch." Mr. Robert's hands shook as he forced the words out. "They're running a few tests now. We're just waiting to hear more." By this time, the Martins had joined them along with a few other friends from the party.

"I'm confused. I thought he was going home after the game. Did he leave?"

"We thought he was going to the party, so I'll guess we'll have to ask her." Linda pointed to the strange girl from the football game, who was slouched over in a nearby chair. She seemed fine except for a few scratches on her face.

"Who is she?" Ellie's voice shook. *What was Dylan doing out with some other girl?*

"I don't know, Ellie." Linda hugged her. "We just found out that she was in the car. She's waiting on her parents. We were just about to talk to her when you came."

Stalking over to the girl, Ellie crossed her arms. "What were you doing in a car with my boyfriend?"

A crowd formed behind Ellie. She glanced over her shoulder. *I don't care if they know what's going on. I just want answers, and this girl has them.*

"I didn't know he was your boyfriend until tonight." The girl's almost black eyes watered and she straightened her back. "I thought he was mine."

"What?" Cara gasped. Ellie motioned Cara and Josh to back off. They took a few steps back, giving them an illusion of privacy, but they could still hear every word. Dylan's parents still hovered by Ellie.

"We met this summer, and when he broke up with me two weeks ago, I wanted to ask him why. I tried calling him and texting him, but he never responded. So, I went to the game and saw y'all kissing. I figured perhaps y'all had just gotten together." The girl stood, towering over Ellie. Her mouth dropping open, Ellie took a step back. Dylan had been dating this girl?

"We've been together for years, so I don't know what you're talking about. Dylan would never cheat on me." Ellie's pitch reached rivaled Mariah Carey's highest. "Never. I don't believe you. Maybe he just flirted with you, but he would never call you his girlfriend."

"Then how do you explain him being out with me tonight?" Her blunt words were just as loud and her tone just as annoyed.

I guess only Dylan can answer that question.

"Girls, maybe we can talk about this later." Dylan's dad stepped in.

"We're okay, Mr. Robert. I just want to know." Ellie sat down and motioned for the girl to sit down, but she continued to stand.

"I do too." The girl's voice shook. She had that same look in her eye that Ellie had when she thought of Dylan.

"So, if you saw us kissing at the game, why did you get in his car tonight?" Ellie cut to the chase.

"Well, I wanted to know what was going on, why he would be with someone so soon after breaking up with me." The girl sat down and gripped the sides of her chair. "He agreed to meet with me, and we went for a drive. When he told me you had been his long-time girlfriend and had just been out of town for the summer, I was furious."

"Kinda like I am now." Ellie clenched her hands together.

"I promise you, I never knew. I guess because you were out of town, there were no warning signs. After school started, he told me he was just busy with football, but I wondered why he never invited me to the games." Tears streamed down her face.

"I noticed the same thing...him being distant," Ellie whispered as the waiting room filled with friends from the party. She saw the smirk on Lindsey's face and donned her game face. Just then, the doctor's entrance caught everyone's attention.

Walking back to Dylan's parents, she left the girl in the back of the crowd, alone. *As she should be.*

"How is he?" Dylan's mom grabbed her husband's arm as the doctor motioned Dylan's parents away from the crowd. Mrs. Linda held Ellie's hand as they waited for the news.

"He has a few cracked ribs and a pretty bad gash on his head from hitting the windshield. He dislocated his shoulder too. But all of that will heal. We'll keep him overnight to keep an eye on the head injury." The doctor started to turn away.

Dylan's dad jumped in, "Is it his right shoulder?" Dylan threw with his right arm. What would happen to his future or the team's playoff chances if he couldn't throw?

"No, it's his left, which was on the side of the impact. He'll be sidelined for a few weeks, but his career is far from over." The doctor smiled and left the family with a nurse who offered to take the family to visit him.

"Come with us, Ellie." Linda motioned for Ellie to follow as Dylan's dad relayed the information to the growing crowd. Ellie hesitated. Dylan's *ex-girlfriend* had sat down, put her legs up on the chair, and was resting her head on her knees. Linda followed Ellie's gaze. Linda called across the room, "I think it's better if you go home with your parents, Amelia, and let Dylan call you when he feels better."

Amelia. So, that was her name. It wasn't her fault Dylan lied, but after she saw Dylan and Ellie kissing at the game, she should have walked away. She got what she deserved chasing after him tonight. As she followed Dylan's parents, the football coach asked everyone to join hands to pray for a quick recovery.

When they arrived at his room, Dylan's parents hurried over, each taking a side. His mom started crying, but his dad started lecturing him. "What were you thinking? You could have ruined your career!"

Who cares about Dylan's football career? She had a hundred questions, none of them related to football.

"That's not what's important now, Robert. He's okay, and we need to be thankful." Linda walked around to her husband's side and put her hand on his arm.

Ellie hovered near the door, leaning against the frame. She might fall over without it. Amelia's words echoed, "I thought he was mine." Everyone knew Dylan had been Ellie's since, well, forever. What was happening? *Mom's cancer and now this. What did I do to deserve this?* She gritted her teeth and turned to walk out.

"Ellie." His voice was weak. She paused in the doorway. "I'm so sorry. Mom, Dad, I'm so sorry. I just lost control of the car. I hadn't been feeling good and couldn't focus."

He wasn't addressing the elephant in the room.

"You should be sorry, Dylan." Ellie marched over to the bed. "That girl told me you were her boyfriend. What's going on?"

"I broke up with her, Ellie. It's you I want." Dylan's eyes welled up. In all the years they had been friends, he had never cried in front of her. Not even the time he broke his leg after jumping out of a tree and had to wait for Ellie to run and get help.

"But, you dated her while I was gone. I can't believe it." Ellie started pacing, her hands clenching.

"You were mad at me when you left. I guess I was mad too." Dylan tried to sit up but fell back on the pillows.

"I don't think this is the best time to talk about it. You need to get your strength back, Dylan." Linda patted his hand.

Ellie rolled her eyes. "When you're mad at me, you go for a run, go boxing with the guys. Heck, you can even flirt with some girl. But, you don't cheat on the girl you love." Ellie paused. "Unless you don't love her."

Dylan held out his good arm toward her, but she stayed put. He started to reply but was cut off by the nurse, who came to give Dylan more pain medicine. He tried to wave her away. "I need to finish this conversation, Miss."

"No, take your medicine, Dylan. We're done talking. We're done period." Ellie held her head up high as she marched out the door, but as soon as she rounded the corner down the hall, she collapsed on the floor, her shoulders shaking as she gasped for air between her silent sobs. She took out her phone and sent a text, asking her dad to pick her up from the hospital.

He replied a minute later. I heard about Dylan. Wanted to let your mom fall asleep before coming. On my way now. Hang tight, sweet girl.

At least there was one guy who wouldn't let her down. As she struggled to stand up, a hand grabbed her arm. Josh and Cara were there.

"We didn't want you to be alone." Cara pulled Ellie up and hugged her.

Keeping her arm around Ellie, Cara guided her to the hospital's front door, giving Josh their purses to hold.

"He's a fool." Anger flashed in Josh's eyes.

Wow, he sounds as bitter as I am. But at least someone's on my side.

"Now's not the time, J." Cara warned.

"I just can't believe it. Dylan's parents didn't even say anything about his cheating. I go back and forth from being so furious that I want to hit him or her or both, to being glad he's not hurt." Ellie sat down on the bench outside the hospital. The crowd had dispersed. "Thanks for staying."

"There's nowhere else we'd rather be. Well, maybe other places we'd rather be, but not when you need us." Cara stroked Ellie's hair, like a mother would do to a sick child.

"I would never have thought he would do this to me." The tears came back, and she leaned her head on Cara's shoulders. Josh paced, his jaw clenched and a deep scowl on his face. Ellie relayed the conversation with Amelia, and the more she talked, the faster Josh walked.

Her dad's car screeched to a halt in front of them, and he ran to embrace Ellie. With his arms around her, she took a long shuddering breath. Her dad would make sure things were okay. He opened the passenger door and addressed the twins. "Thanks for staying with her."

Cara filled Ellie's dad in while Ellie rested in the car. His back was to her, but his shoulders tensed up just like when he was screaming at the referee on TV during a football game. This was going to affect more than just her and Dylan. Just a few weeks ago the two families had gotten together for barbeque. She and her mom had joked that it seemed like the two families were already one. Not anymore.

Josh quit pacing and knocked on her window. She opened her door. "You okay, Lansing?"

"What am I going to do? It's too much. My mom and now Dylan. He's been my world since I first realized boys didn't have cooties." Ellie's chest constricted, but her body was out of tears.

"Maybe that's been the problem. You've been living his life and not your own." Josh put his hand on hers, but she pulled away.

"What a stupid thing to say. We've planned our life together since we first fell in love. You really know how to comfort someone. Maybe you should be a counselor." Her voice dripped with venom, but Josh didn't back away.

"I shouldn't have said that now. I think it's true, but you're right, this isn't the time. Know I'll be praying for you, that God will give you peace." His voice stayed even and steady.

"You told me the other day that he wasn't good enough for me. But I guess I wasn't good enough for him. I couldn't keep his attention." Ellie bent over, cupping her face in her hands.

Josh tilted her head and looked into her eyes. "This is not your fault, Lansing. Dylan's an idiot not to know what he had in front of him." Josh's fingers, calloused from his side job mowing lawns, caressed her arm.

"You left me standing alone on a stage with hundreds of people staring. I guess I'm just not worth sticking around for." Ellie pulled back, and Josh dropped his hands to his side. Her dad opened the driver's side door and slid in, ending the conversation.

Josh leaned into the car to shake her dad's hand and whispered for her ears only, "You're worth the world, Lansing. One day you'll see it." Josh withdrew and stood by Cara as Ellie's dad drove away.

"How are you?" Her dad took her hand and held it as she cried all the way home. With her head resting on the window, Ellie's dad prayed for her. But, this time, it wasn't enough to ease her pain.

Her mom called out as soon as they came through the door. "What happened? Come here."

"I thought you said she was asleep. I don't want Mom worrying about all this right now."

"I sent her a text in case she woke up and wondered where we were. She can handle it. Don't hide your feelings." After giving Ellie a kiss on the forehead, he headed to the den where video game noise signaled that Nick was still awake.

Ellie stumbled into her parents' room and embraced her mom as much as she could. Ellie stretched out beside her mom and told her everything. Just as she finished, her dad came in the room. He took off her shoes for her and told her to stay there, that he would sleep on the couch.

Ellie let her head fall into the soft pillow. Her mom's arm rested on hers as she fell asleep.

12

Ellie awoke the next morning to her mom's raised voice. *What's going on? I've never heard Mom yell before.*

"Linda, I can't believe Dylan would cheat on Ellie. What happened?"

Ellie held still and kept her eyes closed as if she was still sleeping. So, last night wasn't just a bad dream. *Ugh, I don't have the energy to deal with this right now.*

Her mom continued, "I know he's not a bad kid, but I just can't believe he did this. Of course, you should defend your son, but not when he was clearly wrong."

Ellie "woke up" when her mother threw the phone on the bed. "What's going on, Mom?"

"What's going on is that Linda just hung up on me. After what her son did, she should have him out of that bed and here apologizing to you, begging you to forgive him."

Ellie raised her eyebrows. Her mom's outburst would have been funny, something she and Dylan would have imitated later, if it didn't center around her broken heart.

"Mom, I've never seen you so upset. You're supposed to be resting. Lie down." Ellie sat up and took over as nurse. "You'll rip your stitches or something. I can't take Dy... him and you at once." Lying back down, she curled up, bringing her knees to her chest and let out a weak scream.

Instead of reprimanding her for being so emotional, her mom whispered, "Get it all out, and then you can move on." For the next thirty minutes, she and her mom cried together, the first time her mom had not simply told her to get it together and to put on her happy face.

When Ellie opened her eyes, her dad was holding out a box of tissue. "It's too much for a man to see both his girls crying."

He gave Ellie a kiss on her head and his wife one on the lips. "I bought donuts. Let's go eat."

Ellie plodded down the stairs while her dad stayed to help her mom ease out of bed. Nick was at the dining room table. He jumped up and gave Ellie a hug. She took advantage of his rare display of affection and gave him a long embrace.

"You stink, Ellie." He pulled away and held his nose.

Ellie laughed. "Now you know how I've felt since you were born. I'll shower later."

"What he did is all over social media. No one can believe he'd do that to you. I wish his other arm had been hurt so that he wouldn't be able to play football." Nick kept ranting, calling Dylan names that would make their mom threaten to wash his mouth out with soap. Her parents made it down the stairs, ending Nick's tirade. Ellie wouldn't run to check her phone yet. Perhaps if she ignored it, the whole situation would go away.

Her parents sat down at the table.

"Let's pray," her dad suggested. He held out one hand to Ellie and the other to Nick. He prayed for Ellie and his wife, and he ended his prayer asking for Dylan to heal quickly and for God to have His will with their futures.

"Dad, why would you pray for that jerk? Ellie would be stupid to forgive him." Nick shoved a donut in his mouth.

"Forgiveness is a command from the Bible. Whether Ellie chooses to remain friends with him is her choice, but I do pray she will forgive him." Ellie's dad turned to face her. "Unforgiveness will only hurt you in the end."

"I already miss him." Ellie nibbled a donut. "I'm so mad, but I already feel like I'm not me without him, like I'm just half of a whole."

"Ellie, you are whole in Christ, not Dylan." Her mom tried to rub Ellie's arm, but she pulled away.

"Don't give me that church stuff, Mom. I've done everything God asked me to do. I don't cheat at school. I always do everything you and Dad tell me to do. I don't drink, smoke, or do drugs. I didn't even have sex with Dylan when he wanted me to because I knew that was against God's rules." Ellie stood up and threw her napkin on the table. "Where did following His orders get me? A mom who could die of cancer and a boyfriend who cheated. Just let me be mad for one day before telling me how your perfect daughter should act." Ellie left her family with stunned expressions as she stomped up the stairs to her bedroom.

In her room, she plugged her dead phone into the charger. Taking out some fresh pajamas, she headed to the bathroom to take a shower. She stood under the hot water until her skinned burned more than the pain in her heart.

Dressed in pajamas, she returned to her room. Her dad had stuck a note to her door. *We're sorry for telling you how to react. We love you and are here for you, no matter how you feel.* She wrote back on his note. *I know. Love you both. I'm going to go back to sleep.* Locking her door, she put on her headphones, cranked up the music, and checked the text messages on her phone.

Thirty-five texts, most from friends who couldn't believe what was happening. Cara had sent her one last night and then again this morning, saying she was there for her. A few football players sent texts telling her Dylan would be staying in the hospital after they were done with him. She smiled a little. The final one was from a number she didn't have in her phone.

`Check your mailbox.`

Texting Nick, she asked him to go check the mailbox. He bounded up the stairs and pounded on her door a minute later.

"Thanks, Nick. You're the best." Ellie tried to give him a hug, but he pulled away. She should have known better than to expect two hugs in one day.

"Can I see what it is?" Nick sat on her bed and waited for her to open the envelope.

"Yeah. I don't know who it could be. I didn't recognize the number." When Ellie pulled out the index card, she knew what it was. "My scripture drop."

"What? Just an index card?"

"After we found out about Mom's cancer, someone started leaving me scriptures on cards in my locker. I guess they've started delivering them here too." Ellie read the scripture aloud. "Come to me, all you who are weary and burdened, and I will give you rest. Take my yoke upon you and learn from me, for I am gentle and humble in heart, and you will find rest for your souls. For my yoke is easy and my burden is light. Matthew 11: 28-30."

Her muscles relaxed with each of the precious words. Her scripture dropper had supported her multiple times a day with verses when her mom was sick. Since the surgery's success, they had decreased to just one a day, but she still checked her locker for a new note between each class.

Nick wrinkled his nose, gave her an awkward pat on the back, and left. Ellie locked her door again and sent a text to her anonymous friend. Thank you so much for the scripture. Who is this?

The reply came back within a couple minutes. Just a friend who wants to see you happy.

The way I feel now, I don't think I ever will be again. But, I do appreciate all the notes after my mom was diagnosed. You don't know how much those cards meant to me. I have them in my journal.

The pink sequined one we all teased you about when you wrote down the scriptures in youth group?

How'd you know?

I wrote them down too. That's where I've been pulling the scriptures for the cards.

Ok, so we go to church together. We must be friends. How come I don't have you in my phone? This is a little weird. Just tell me who you are.

There was no reply for thirty minutes.

I just wanted to encourage you, for you to see yourself the way I do. I didn't want you to know who I am because it may make things weirder than they already are. Check your mailbox again.

Ellie opened the door. Her dad had added to the note taped on her door. *Went to Nick's football game. Your mom took some pain medicine and will be asleep for a while. We'll be home right after the game.*

Good. She could check the mailbox without anyone noticing. She glanced at her orange shorts and yellow and purple tank top, then shrugged and raced outside. She opened the mailbox and pulled out a folded sheet of paper. It was a thicker paper than normal computer paper.

She unfolded the paper and gasped. It was the drawing she had seen in Josh's sketchbook, the one of the girl sitting on a surfboard, riding the waves. In the gray sky, he had written a scripture. "When thou passest through the waters, I will be with thee; and through the rivers, they shall not overflow thee: when thou walkest through the fire, thou shalt not be burned; neither shall the flame kindle upon thee. Isaiah 43:2"

It looked like the old King James version that was too hard to read, but the words had a poetic cadence. She leaned against the brick mailbox and clutched the paper to her chest. Her gaze darted around. Was Josh watching her from somewhere nearby? His jeep wasn't in sight, so she headed back inside. There was a text waiting for her.

What did you think?

It's beautiful. Thanks, Josh. I've been so mean to you lately, but you've been amazing. Thanks for all of the cards.

I deserved it. By the way, great pajamas. I should've taken a picture to blackmail you.

So you were there. If you hadn't been so nice, I would call you a creepy stalker.

Just watching out for you.

Josh was very protective of Cara. Maybe he felt he should protect her too. Ellie set the phone aside. She took a photo of her and Dylan out of a large frame and trimmed the edge of Josh's sketch to make it fit. She took a picture of the framed drawing, sent it to Josh and posted it online. Her friends would know she would be okay. Probably not today, but one day.

Planning to spend the rest of the day in her pajamas, listening to Taylor Swift break-up songs and eating Reece's peanut butter cups, Ellie curled up in her bed, checking her phone to see if Cara had texted. Instead, there was a text from Dylan.

Don't hate me. I do love you.

He always knows the right words to say, but I'm not going to fall for it this time. Deleting the message, she leaned back on her pillows, watching the ceiling fan swirl around. Suddenly, she sat up. "Dang it," she muttered. Tonight was homecoming. And she was homecoming queen. The football game was a lifetime ago, back when she was naïve Ellie who believed her world was perfect.

Jumping out of bed, Ellie rummaged in her closet. Where was the costume they had put together when the "50s" theme had been announced? *Ah, here we go.* She pulled it out and held it up to her body. The soft pink circle skirt skimmed her legs. So much for Dylan twirling her around the dance floor. He loved to dance and was good at it, just as smooth as he was on the football field. *Guess he can add lying to that list of talents. He should put that on his applications to colleges he never mentioned to me.*

Everyone would be talking about what happened last night. She might as well let them see her and get all their gossip out before the school week. *I'll show them that I'm stronger than they thought. Stronger than I think I am.* She would put on her happy face and pretend all was fine. It was what her mother did every day. Even when grandmother had passed away, Ellie's mom had allowed herself to cry just one day. The next morning, she was back to her polished appearance, telling the family it was time to get back to normal. Her mom would tell her to get back out there and show the world she was better than ok. Besides, her classmates had voted her homecoming queen, and that meant something. Showing up would tell them how much she appreciated their support.

Ellie sent a text to Cara to say she was going to the dance and would love to ride with her. Cara replied that she would pick her up. Ellie had three hours to kill before she needed to get ready.

On her desk was the picture of her and Dylan that she had taken out of the frame. It had been taken the Christmas Dylan was three and Ellie still two. Their parents had been trying to get a cute picture of them by the tree, but a rambunctious Dylan had other plans. His little hands gripped the tree branches and shook, making the glitter fall like snow. He was grinning and looking up at the glitter while Ellie stared at Dylan in shock. Even then, Dylan had been finding adventures while she stood with eyes only for him. Ellie's mom would tell her that following the man you love is nothing to be ashamed of, but her dad would tell Ellie to forge her own path. Which one was right?

Ellie laid all of the framed pictures of Dylan face down. They contained most of her life's memories, but she would lose her mind sitting in that room staring at them, the happier times haunting her. Then she checked on her mom, who was still in a deep sleep. Her mom would be mortified if people could see her when she slept. It was the only time she let her guard down. Her hair was sticking out, her mouth open, and even a little drool escaped to her pillow. Ellie kissed her cheek and tucked the quilt up around her arms, careful to avoid her stitches.

Grabbing a book, Ellie took a long bubble bath with lavender aromatherapy bath salts and a few candles added for good measure. Jenny B. Jones' sarcastic heroine and a long soak were exactly what she needed to relax.

Back in her room and hour later, she plugged in her flat iron to warm up and then froze. For years, she had spent hours straightening her hair when Dylan was the only one who liked it that way. Well, now he had a new girl with hair as straight as a board, and Ellie could do whatever she wanted with her hair. Ellie played with different styles before settling on a low bun with a few curls falling down around her face.

Dressed, Ellie looked at the stranger in the mirror. Her smile didn't quite reach her eyes, and her hands shook a little as she readjusted the polka-dotted scarf tied around her neck. She wore a little more make-up than normal. Hopefully no one else would notice her puffy red eyes. People would be watching her, but perhaps it would be too dark to see details. The front door thudded shut and she went downstairs. Her dad and Nick had just walked in.

"You are beautiful." Her dad paused. "Are you sure you want to go tonight? Everyone will understand if you want to stay home."

"You should go, Ellie." Defiance was written all over Nick's face. "Don't let that loser keep you from having fun."

"I wish it was that easy, Nick, but you're right. I was voted queen, so I should go." Ellie's voice shook. What was she thinking getting dressed up for a couple hundred people to stare at and analyze her every move?

"Well, you know your mom would applaud you for getting back out there and not letting them see you sweat. Wait there." Their dad raced up the stairs.

"How was the game? I'm sorry I missed it." She followed Nick into the kitchen.

"It was awesome. My best game ever. I pictured their quarterback as Dylan and had three sacks and four tackles for losses." Nick grinned as he opened the fridge and pulled out some milk.

"Aww, that is really great. I'll be back next week."

Their dad bounded down the stairs. He held a strand of pearls, her mom's beloved necklace. Ellie's great-great-grandmother had given the necklace to Ellie's mother, who promised to pass it on to Ellie's daughter one day. Ellie used to beg to borrow the pearls, but her mom always said Ellie wasn't quite old enough. "These will be perfect. You're almost an adult, and I couldn't be more proud to be your dad."

Ellie took off the scarf, and her dad fastened the clasp. She fingered her mom's prized possession, pearls that had graced three, now four, generations of women. "It's perfect, Dad. I love it."

She gave him a hug. He kissed her hair and told her to go to the stairs for a few pictures. Tying the scarf around her wrist, she pasted on a smile and posed for her dad and Nick, who tried his best to make her laugh by doing crazy dances behind her dad's back.

When Cara arrived, they took more pictures, and then the two girls were off. Ellie checked her phone once they were in the car. Again, there was a text from Dylan.

`I saw the picture you posted. I guess it didn't take long for another picture to replace mine.`

So, he can date another girl while I'm out of town, but I can't change a picture in a frame?

She deleted his text without responding. Before she could put the phone back in her purse, another text arrived. Dylan again.

`Sorry. That's not what I meant. I'm just frustrated you won't text or call me, and I'm stuck in this hospital bed.`

Why hadn't he been released yet? Maybe this was all a mistake and they could get through it. Maybe. But she wouldn't text him back just yet.

"Let him sweat it out, Ellie." Cara must have read her mind. As she stared out of the window, Ellie told Cara about the texts.

"I'm so mad at him, but that doesn't stop my heart from loving him. It's like I don't know how to do anything else but love him. Would it be crazy for me to forgive him?"

"I wouldn't, but I've never been in love. You hear about couples who forgive cheating, but it seems they have more to fight for."

"More than a lifelong love?"

"Well, a marriage, kids, a family."

"You're probably right. That's why I didn't text back. I don't know what to say. My heart is broken. And I'm so mad. But I still can't imagine a life without him."

"Well, know I'm here for you no matter what you decide." They pulled into the parking lot, and Ellie hesitated before opening her door. "You are stronger than you know, Eleanor Rebecca Lansing, but you don't have to go to the dance tonight. We can go back to my house and throw darts at pictures of Dylan."

"While that sounds therapeutic, I need to do this." A few minutes later, Ellie paused at the front door of the school. The music was loud enough to drown out the sound of her throbbing heart and the lights would be low enough to hide her shaking hands. Taking a deep breath, she opened the doors and walked through.

The girls had planned to arrive fashionably late, sneaking in unnoticed. But that wasn't going to happen. Time froze as Ellie stared at the crowd. What was she thinking showing up? *I should have stayed home.*

Her chest tightened. *I will not let them see me cry.* She turned to beg Cara to do something, but Cara had been stopped by the teacher at the door. Suddenly, Josh stood before her, bowing his head and stretching out his hand. She grabbed it.

"Students of Waltham Christian Academy, I present Queen Ellie." He let her hand go and bowed dramatically, eliciting a few cheers and a round of applause. "Back to your festivities." Josh motioned with his hand for them to return to their dancing and eating.

"Thanks for rescuing me, Josh. I'm wondering if this was a good idea." Ellie's hands shook.

"You're worth rescuing, Lansing. I've always wanted to save a damsel in distress."

"I'll show you damsel in distress." Ellie dug in her clutch and pulled out the mace her dad insisted she carry everywhere.

"I surrender." Josh laughed and backed away. "You win. You could take me."

"And don't forget it." Ellie smiled for the first time since walking through the door.

Lindsey sauntered up to Josh and linked her arm through his. Lindsey had been talking about how hot Josh was at the football game. She must have gotten what she wanted. "Hi, Ellie. I'm surprised you would show up here after last night."

"Knock it off, Lindsey. We couldn't have a homecoming without the queen." Josh started to run his fingers through his short hair, getting rid of Lindsey's arm, and paused when he hit a wall of hair gel that protected his 1950s-style slick over.

"Greaser." Ellie teased.

"And you are looking like a Soc," Josh retorted.

"Yes, we've all read *The Outsiders*. We've got a real Ponyboy and Cherry here. Next, y'all will be talking about the sunset." Lindsey rolled her eyes. "Let's go dance, Josh."

Giving Ellie a shrug, Josh followed Lindsey out onto the dance floor.

Cara came up behind Ellie. "You know he came with her because her mom called our mom and gave her some sob story about Lindsey's date getting a stomach bug and Lindsey was going to have to come alone. Come on, let's get a Coke."

"I was wondering. I know she's aggressive when she stalks her prey." Ellie poured a drink for herself and took a sip.

Cara laughed. "Mom fell for it, and I think Josh just wanted to make Mom happy. She's been after him to have some fun. He wasn't in the mood to come tonight but thought he should since he's homecoming king and all."

Ellie and Cara made small talk about the decorations and the costumes. Although Lindsey kept trying to drape her arms around Josh's neck, he kept standing back and dancing in a group. He was a goofy dancer with no rhythm and he didn't quite know what to do with his arms.

Cara pointed at Josh. "He's horrible. How can he run so gracefully on the football field and move like a robot on speed on the dance floor?"

Ellie laughed, and they started counting the times Josh stepped on Lindsey's foot, taking turns guessing what Lindsey was thinking as she tried to slow dance with him while he bobbed around.

After the third time Ellie caught Josh looking her way, she gave him a smile. He was sweet to check on her. After Dylan's treachery, Josh's betrayal last spring was miniscule.

Ellie fiddled with her pearl necklace while they sat in a comfortable silence. Cara was focused on a certain guy across the gym, who was chatting with some of the football team.

"Who caught your eye at last?" Ellie giggled when Cara jerked to attention.

"Do you know him? He transferred here from North Carolina. His name is Mark something. He came over the other day with J, and I realized I hadn't ever seen him on campus."

"It's okay to be interested in a guy, Cara."

"Who said I was interested? I'm just trying to be a servant of Christ, reaching out to the new student who had the misfortune of starting a new school during senior year." Cara's face grew bright red. "I don't know, Ellie. I've never felt this way. I got so nervous talking to him. J was laughing at me while I tried to ask him questions. I couldn't form a complete sentence." Cara took a sip of her drink.

"Go dance with him. Be friendly." Ellie stood and motioned Cara to stand up. "Don't forget that verse that says to greet each other with a holy kiss."

Cara stayed seated. "You're crazy. It was enough for me to admit I think he's cute. I'll let him pursue me. If he even remembers me."

"Okay, I get that. A man is made to chase women. Remember when Mrs. Gramble gave us that speech?"

Cara laughed. "How I could forget? We were all drawing pictures of cheetahs with guys' faces on them." Ellie laughed too.

Mark materialized in front of them. "Hi, Cara. Would you like to dance?"

The music had switched to a slow ballad, and couples were beginning to pair off. Ellie jabbed Cara in the back when she didn't answer.

"Sure." Cara gave a tiny smile as she took Mark's hand.

"Let that cheetah catch you," Ellie whispered as she took Cara's clutch. Ellie's first dance with Dylan had been in this very room. It had been as magical as a middle school dance in the school gym could be, and Ellie had been a princess in his arms. It was also the first time her parents had let her wear heels, and she had taken them off after the first dance, letting her dress swish against the floor. *Will I ever feel that way again?*

"Looking for me?" Josh plopped down in Cara's seat.

"Don't get a big head." Ellie laughed.

"So, you were looking for me then. Well, I'm right here."

"I'm shocked Lindsey let you out of her death grip. You know she's into you, right?"

"That doesn't mean I'm into her. Her date got sick, and she didn't want to come alone. I didn't have a date, so I agreed." He grinned and leaned forward like he was going to tell her a secret. "My mom may have convinced me by promising some art supplies. But, you didn't hear that from me."

"Hey, why you came with her is your business, not mine."

"I want you to know, Lansing." Josh looked back to the crowd.

"And now I do."

Josh held up his empty drink to indicate he was going to get a refill. He returned a minute later with two full cups.

Just then, the principal tapped the mike and announced it was time to present the queen and king. Although everyone knew who the winners were, at the dance they were presented to the school body, crowned, and led the rest of the court in a dance.

"That's our cue. Ready to twirl?" Josh set down the drinks and led Ellie to the sidelines to wait their turn on the stage.

After the freshman, sophomore, and junior court members were introduced, the principal announced, "And to represent the senior class as queen, Eleanor Lansing."

Ellie took a deep breath and walked to the front to get her crown again. Tears came to her eyes as the crowd clapped and whistled.

"Joining her as king is Joshua Martin." Josh did a little dance on his way, getting everyone to laugh. "And now, they will lead the court in a dance."

Taking her hand, Josh led Ellie out onto the dance floor as the song began. Everyone was staring at her. This had better be different from the last time she and Josh shared the spotlight.

"I'm not going to walk away this time. You can relax. You can trust me not to hurt you again."

"I'm just worried about you hurting my toes," Ellie joked. Over a hundred people were watching and taking photos. After the first chorus, Ellie took a deep breath and rested her head on his chest. The dance ended way too soon, but Josh didn't let go of her right away, holding on to her until she pulled away. "Thanks, Joshua."

"Anytime, Lansing. Can we do it again?"

"Yeah, if Lindsey will let you out of her clutches."

"I'll start planning my escape now." Josh tucked a curl behind her ear. "Glad to see you're back to your curls. They're pretty on you."

Lindsey appeared and grabbed Josh's hand, pulling him to dance to the fast song that was playing. Ellie raised her voice, "Thanks for letting me borrow him."

"You can borrow me any time. Why don't you dance with us?" He tried to pull her into the group. Cara and Mark were also dancing in the group, so Ellie joined in, but she avoided Josh so as to not make waves with Lindsey.

After dancing up a storm for an hour, Ellie took a bathroom break. Tucked in a stall, the gossip caught up to her.

"I can't believe she showed up here after what we all saw and heard last night."

"I kinda admire her for it. Maybe she's stronger than we all thought she was. I would have hidden for a few weeks."

"I think she'll take him back. Weak girls always do."

"Maybe she'll move on. She and Josh looked cute dancing. Speaking of dancing, let's go."

Ellie waited until the two girls left before coming out of the stall. They had perfectly expressed the tug-of-war in her heart, besides the Josh thing of course.

She checked her phone. There was a text from her dad, asking how it was going, but nothing from Dylan. She typed a quick reply to her dad and rejoined the party. A slow song was playing. Xavier came up and asked if he could dance with her.

"Sure, if it's okay with Amanda." After making Lindsey mad, the last thing she needed was to upset any other girls.

"Yeah, girl, I'm going to get something to drink. Y'all have fun." Amanda gave her an encouraging smile as she walked toward the punch fountain.

As they swayed to the music, Xavier cut to the chase. "Dylan is an idiot to do that to you, and I know he's my friend, but I threatened to put him back in the hospital if he ever does anything close to that again. But, you need to know he's sorry. His head wound got infected, so I guess he's getting what he deserves."

"I guess. I want to hate him, but I can't. That doesn't mean I want him back, but I wish this all would go away."

Maybe that girl is right. I am weak, still loving him after he broke my heart.

"Well, he said he's willing to do whatever it takes to get you back." Xavier gave her one more twirl as the song ended and they walked back to Amanda.

"He's all yours, Amanda. Enjoy. He's a good guy." Ellie gave Amanda a quick hug, then Xavier and Amanda wrapped their arms around each other for another slow song.

Ellie sat at the table. Her mom would be proud of her for putting on her big girl britches and showing up tonight. She hadn't cried, which had to be considered a success. She spent the rest of the evening chatting with friends who came by to say hello and watching Cara dance with Mark, who had been her partner for almost every song. As the DJ announced the last song, another ballad, Ellie went to the courtyard and sat next to the fountain.

"We seem to find ourselves next to water often." Josh sat down next to her.

"Just enjoying a little peace and quiet." Maybe he would get the hint. He did, settling in to sit next to her, listening to the fountain in silence. When the DJ announced the dance was over, Josh stood up and handed her a quarter.

"Let's make a wish and throw it in the fountain. It will make someone who forgets his lunch money on Monday very happy." Josh held up three quarters. "You can have two if you want."

Ellie took another one. She closed her eyes, made a wish that her mom would be okay, and then tossed the quarter over her shoulder into the pool of water. It hit the water with a plop.

"You have one more. Make it count." Josh had already tossed his before Ellie had even finished making her wish.

"You must have known what you wanted to wish for. I wished my mom would be okay, but I'm not sure what to wish for this one."

"You're not supposed to tell people what the wish is. That ruins it." Josh shook his head. "But, that's a good wish."

"Thanks." *Should I wish Dylan and I will make up, or not?* Finally, she wished to be happy and threw her second coin in the water. "I hope your wish comes true."

"Well, if you would tell me what your second one was, I would tell you if I hope it comes true." Josh put his arm on her shoulder as they headed back to the party.

"You just told me I shouldn't tell you."

"Well, I changed my mind."

"That's only a woman's prerogative." Ellie smiled as they came to a stop next to one of the pillars at the edge of the garden. "But, I'll tell you if you tell me."

"I wished for you to find peace." Josh's tone was serious as he looked at Ellie, past the happy face she had worn for the last two hours to the real her that wasn't sure what she was going to do.

"You shouldn't have wasted your wish on me."

"Wasn't wasted. That was just one wish. Now, what was yours?"

"I see Lindsey searching for you. I'm sure she's eager to make all your wishes come true." Ellie gave him a punch on the arm, dodging the question.

He rubbed his arm like her punch hurt. "Nah. I told her she's just a friend. I think she wants a boyfriend more than she wants me." Josh started walking toward Lindsey but spun back to give her one more look. "See you later, Lansing."

Later that night as she lay back on her bed, she replayed the night's events. She and Cara had talked until two in the morning about Mark, Dylan, and even her renewed friendship, perhaps better called talkship, with Josh. Cara had fallen asleep mid-sentence, but now at four a.m., sleep still eluded Ellie.

Within two weeks, her world had been rocked, and the very person she would usually turn to was the reason for her broken heart. She tried to pray, but all that would come out was hurt that God was taking away the people she loved most. The scriptures that had brought peace earlier now seemed to taunt her. What good was doing the right thing if life was still going to be hard? The answer didn't come, but the whirl of the spinning fan blades lulled her to sleep.

13

Dylan sent apology text messages every day. Ellie ignored them for six days. But she couldn't ignore him forever. The gossip loop said he was out of the hospital but wouldn't be back at school until next week. What should she say to him when she saw him again? Arriving home from youth group Wednesday night, Ellie gasped. Dylan's parents' car was in her driveway.

Ellie hesitated before getting out. Dylan's parents would take her side to an extent, but he was still their son. Her heart raced. She climbed out but stopped in her tracks. Dylan was sitting in one of the porch lounge chairs. The conflict she had been avoiding had just shown up at her front door.

He stood and started to walk toward her. Ellie stood frozen, letting him take the lead.

"Hey, Ellie." What a pitiful sight. He still had a bandage on his forehead, his face was bruised, and his arm was in a sling. She searched his eyes for answers to the questions she couldn't even ask. "I'm so sorry. I don't know what else to say."

"I don't know what to say either, Dylan." Tears flowed down her cheeks. "Part of me wants to hit you, and the other part of me is so thankful you weren't hurt worse. Then I go back to thinking you deserve whatever pain you are in."

Dylan inched closer, and when she didn't back away, he moved close enough to touch, although she didn't. "I deserve it all. I can't believe I was so stupid."

"Why, Dylan? Why would you cheat on me?" Ellie walked to the porch chairs. Her legs might not hold her when he answered.

"I don't know." Dylan pulled up a chair facing her and sat.

"Don't give me that lame excuse, Dylan. I deserve more than that." Ellie rolled her eyes and ran her fingers through her hair.

"I guess I just felt under a lot of pressure. One of my earliest memories is of my mom telling me one day I would marry you. We dressed up as a groom and bride for Halloween when we were seven. Our moms planned our lives out from elementary to where we would go to college to where our honeymoon would be." Dylan stood and picked at the porch rail's peeling paint. "Don't you ever feel trapped?"

"You felt trapped with me?" Ellie shrank back into her chair. *Why can't he even look at me while he talks?*

"No, not by you. But by the plan. How many times did you hear about the plan, Ellie?"

"A lot." Ellie had to admit the truth.

"I felt I couldn't breathe. Every step is planned out for me, and I wanted to escape. I didn't want to think about college, marriage, and kids. I just wanted to have fun swimming, playing football, and being 17." He paused and looked down at her for a split second before returning his gaze to the paint.

"And she helped you do that?" It was hard to breathe. Wasn't she enough for him?

"No, well, yes, I guess. She didn't have a plan, didn't need a life-long commitment. I could just be carefree." Dylan sat, staring at the ground instead of her. When she didn't respond, he leaned back in his chair, his face pale.

Was he was about to pass out? Ellie reached to put her hand on his arm but pulled back just before they touched. "Are you okay?"

"No, I'm not, Ellie. I screwed up. I wanted freedom from my parents' expectations, not from loving you. Now, I've lost you and possibly my football career." A tear slid down his purple cheek.

Is that tear for losing me? Or for losing a football career?

"Dylan, you could have told me this."

"You were in Nantucket, and when we did talk, it was always about how great senior year was going to be or where we should apply to college."

"Then why didn't you just break up with me?" She was starting to scream. "You were everything to me, Dylan. Everything. My whole world revolved around you."

"Maybe that added to the expectations I felt I had to live up to." Dylan shook his head.

"So, now this is my fault? I can't believe what I'm hearing." Ellie stood and grabbed her bag. She didn't have to stick around for this.

"No, I'm the jerk. You are the perfect Ellie Lansing everyone loves."

Ellie's heart ripped open at the same moment her blood boiled.

"Well, obviously you don't. You have no idea what I've been going through. My world is shaken to the core, Dylan. My mom's cancer, and now this." Ellie's voice shook. Tears streamed down her face. She stood in front of him until he looked her in the eye.

"I'm so sorry. What can I do to make it up to you?" Dylan reached to touch her hand, but she crossed her arms.

"You know what the very worst part is? It's that the one person I want to comfort me, the person who I go to with every hurt is *you*. I have all this anger and hurt, and you're the person who is always there to make things better and now you're the one causing me the pain." Ellie collapsed into the chair and buried her face in her hands.

Dylan got on his knees and wrapped his good arm around her. "I'm so sorry, Ellie. So, so sorry."

Ellie let him hold her. It would be the last time. Putting her head on his familiar shoulder, she cried for the loss of her first love and her longest friendship. When his hot tears fell on her face, she opened her eyes. Pain was etched on his face. His eyes were closed. His sorrow was evident. What did he expect to happen now? Did he expect her to move on as if nothing happened? Did he want them to "be friends?" Or were they going to go their separate ways forever, becoming tidbits of news passed along between their moms?

What do I want to happen next?

Ellie leaned back in the chair, and Dylan stayed on his knees in front of her. "I love you, Ellie, and I will do anything to earn your trust again. I want you to forgive me. I know you're still mad now, but I'll be here waiting on you when you think you can trust me."

Dylan put his hand on her arm, and this time she let him. "I'm not giving up on us. The last few days have been horrible. Even though I felt pressured by the plan, you were the best part of it. I don't care about the rest. Just you."

How am I supposed to respond to that? "Have you talked to Amelia again?"

"Just once. I called to say I was sorry for what happened and explained that I loved you and wanted to work things out with you."

"What'd she say?" Ellie couldn't look into his eyes. What if he lied to her again? Or worse, what if he lied and she couldn't tell the difference?

"She was mad that I lied. There were a lot of curse words thrown around, all of which I deserved."

So many questions. How'd they meet? What had they done on dates? When did he first kiss her? Had Dylan told Amelia he loved her? But all that information would only torment her. "Did you have sex with her?"

"No. Of course not." Dylan's blue eyes pierced into her own, but was he telling her the truth? How could she trust anything he said now? "Please believe me. She was nothing but a summer distraction."

Ellie had a lot to say in response to that, but none of it would change what happened. Would it make it better if he had cared for Amelia, that he hadn't thrown away their relationship for a simple distraction?

"Do you think you can ever forgive me? Just try. Promise me you'll try." The desperation in Dylan's voice tugged at Ellie's heart.

"I have to forgive you. It's one of the rules in the Bible. I just don't know when I'll be able to." She would be honest even though he hadn't extended that courtesy to her.

"I'm truly sorry. I felt so bad you found out that way. I thought Martin would have told you the day you got back to town."

"Josh?" Ellie's brow wrinkled. "He knew?"

"I think so."

The pieces all fell together. "The fight? Was it over her?"

"Not over her. He asked me if I was cheating on you, that he had seen me with her. I told him I wasn't, but I don't think he believed me. We were at Connor's party, and he confronted me again. He told me you were too good for me and sucker-punched me." Dylan rubbed his jaw where Josh had hit him.

"That doesn't sound like him."

"I guess when it comes to you, it does." Dylan fidgeted with a string hanging on his sling.

"What does that mean?"

"You know he's always had a crush on you, Ellie. Half of the guys at school do." Dylan smiled for the first time that evening.

"But, he's always known I'm yours." Ellie stopped herself. "Was yours. He told me he had tried to apologize to me after the play. Why didn't you ever tell me?"

"Because I knew he had a crush on you. When y'all were doing the play, I could see the way he looked at you. He used to laugh about you being Cara's uptight friend, but after the first week or so of practices, he wasn't acting." Dylan caught her gaze, and this time Ellie looked away.

"We were never more than friends. I never saw anyone but you. You know that. You shouldn't have kept that from me. I thought he hated me."

"I guess I was jealous and didn't want y'all to be close, and now I've sent you running straight to him. I guess he wins." Dylan picked off a few leaves from the plant on the porch.

Ellie sighed. "Love isn't a competition, Dylan."

"You and I have so much history, so many good memories. I hope you'll forgive me and give me a chance to make it up to you." Dylan took her hand and brought her to her feet. "Let's make new memories."

Ellie rubbed her temples. "I don't know, Dylan." *I wish he'd just kiss me, and we could pretend this never happened. No. I can't.*

"Well, you don't have to decide tonight. I'm not going anywhere. I'm here when you're ready." He picked up her purse from the porch, opened the front door, and followed her into the house.

Their parents were sitting in the living room with solemn faces. Obviously they had just finished a conversation like the one she and Dylan had just had.

Awkward silence. Dylan spoke first.

"Mr. and Mrs. Lansing, I have apologized to Ellie, but I want to say I'm sorry to you as well. I was wrong."

Ellie's dad stood up. "You got that right. I trusted you with one of the most valuable things I have—my daughter's heart. On your first date, you promised to treasure that gift. If it weren't for your parents, I would be in jail for what I want to do to you."

Ellie's mom pulled him down to his seat. "While we're obviously hurt for Ellie, we know you're young, Dylan, and young people make mistakes. I'm glad you see what you did was wrong."

"She's right." Ellie's dad controlled his voice. "My sweet girl, since you were a baby, I wanted to protect your heart from any pain, and I'm sorry I couldn't."

Ellie ran to her dad and let him engulf her in the strong arms that had once carried her. "Thanks, Daddy."

Looking at her mom, Ellie said what her mom wanted to hear. "I'm going to be okay. We're all going to be okay."

Linda spoke up. "Dylan feels horrible, and I hope you'll forgive him."

"Don't put any pressure on her, Linda. What happens next is up to Ellie." Her dad turned Ellie a little so that Linda couldn't see her, as if that would keep her ears from hearing the words.

"I hope this won't change our friendship, Linda, but we'll support whatever decision Ellie makes." Although her mom tried to smooth things over, no one would leave with a happy face — fake or not — tonight.

Mr. Grant stood. "Well, I guess that settles it. Dylan said what he needed to say, and I want to tell Ellie that Linda and I are sorry as well. We didn't know what was going on, or we would have put a stop to it."

Ellie looked at the man who had been a second dad to her.

Mr. Grant continued, "We see you as our girl too, and I'm so sorry you're hurting."

Ellie stood and gave him a hug. Hiding her face in his neck, she whispered, "You'll always be Uncle Robert."

He gave her a kiss on the top of her head and released her, putting his arm around Linda's waist to walk her out.

"I'll be waiting, Ellie. Whenever you're ready." Dylan gave her one last pleading glance before following his parents out the door.

Collapsing into the nearest chair after the door shut, Ellie put her hands over her ears to block out her parents arguing in the den. Her mom wanted Ellie to go back to normal like nothing happened while her dad hoped Ellie would never talk to him again. Gritting her teeth, she got up and went to her room. Silence. She fell onto her bed. She didn't have a single ounce of physical or emotional strength left. *What did Dylan mean that Josh has always had a crush on me?* But she fell asleep half a second later.

14

Friday night came too quickly. The week had been a haze of school, work, cheer practice, and helping take care of her mom, who was finally getting around the house.

She had tried to talk to Josh during English class, but they were doing group projects, so there was little privacy. He said hello, but not much more. And how was she supposed to bring up what Dylan had said? Should she just ask Josh if he had known what was going on this summer? Or ask the real question about whether he had feelings for her, as Dylan believed?

Ellie hadn't seen Dylan since their talk. He wasn't back at school yet, but he would be at the football game to support his teammates. Everyone had been understanding, but why couldn't the whole situation just go away? Lining up with the cheerleaders, Ellie searched for Dylan out of habit. He wasn't in the stands with his parents, who were sitting next to her parents. She smiled. At least her parents hadn't lost their best friends. She had lost hers one week ago, and she would never be the same.

"Hey."

She turned. Dylan was wearing his football jersey with gym shorts. His blue eyes met hers, and butterflies began to flutter in her stomach.

"Hi." Ellie glanced around. Was anyone watching? What gossip would start just from a simple exchange? "How are you feeling?"

"Better. It's killing me not being out on the field." He pointed at Brady Smith, the sophomore backup quarterback. "I was so stupid, but I guess I've got to live with the consequences."

"Yeah." *Oh, no.* Josh was watching them. He looked confused and a little hurt. No matter what she decided to do, she was going to disappoint someone.

"I'm sorry people are staring." Dylan followed Ellie's gaze at Josh. "He's not happy we're working things out, is he?"

"I don't know. I haven't talked to him the last few days, but he's been a good friend the last few weeks." Ellie gave a quick wave to Josh. He replied with a weak smile before turning back to the team.

"Well, thanks for speaking to me. I guess we're making progress." Dylan gave her an awkward pat on the shoulder and joined the team. Her skin sizzled as he walked away. How long would the uncomfortable tension last?

The rest of the squad surrounded Ellie, asking what Dylan said and how Ellie was feeling. "I don't know what to think or even what I feel. I go back and forth twenty times a day between loving him and hating him."

"Better decide soon before he gives up." Of course Lindsey would say that.

"Just shut up, Lindsey." Even Melissa didn't seem in the mood for Lindsey's cattiness.

"I'm not trying to be mean, but guys like Dylan don't wait around forever for a girl to make up her mind." What exactly was she referring to...getting back with Dylan or sleeping with him, or both?

"Thanks, Lindsey, for telling me what you *think*. But, since you can't keep a guy longer than a week, you don't understand how hard it is to walk away from someone you've dated for years and loved since you were a kid." Ellie tightened her ponytail. *Sigh. I don't want to be mean, but I'm not in the mood for jealous snobs.*

The rest of the squad giggled at Ellie's surprising comeback as Coach Robbins strode over and told them to get in formation. Although the Eagles fought hard, they lost by a field goal. Heads bowed, the team sulked off the field. As usual, the cheerleaders waited outside the locker room to cheer them up as they left for their cars. One of the last out, Josh hung out by the door until most of the guys drove off.

"Hey, Lansing, wait up." He jogged toward her, his hair wet from the shower, a frown on his face.

"You played a good game." Maybe she could say something to cheer him up, the way he had helped her.

"My head wasn't in it tonight. I couldn't get you and Dylan talking out of my mind. What are you thinking?" Josh slung his backpack over his shoulder.

"I don't know what I'm thinking. One minute I think I hate him. The next I think that our love is strong enough to overcome anything. I don't know what I think, but everyone is quick to tell me what I should do." Lindsey and Melissa were watching. She turned her back on them. "So, tell me, what's your opinion?" She tried to keep the sarcasm out of her voice but failed.

"You're my friend. You've always been my friend, and he's a jerk. He had the most amazing girl, and he chose to have fun for a summer instead of a lifetime of love. That's stupid. He doesn't deserve you. Can't you see that?" He closed the gap between them with two steps and wrapped her in a hug.

"Did you know?" He didn't answer right away. She kept her head buried in his chest. What if he lied, just like Dylan?

"No. I thought he might be seeing someone else, but I didn't know for sure." Josh pulled away and looked her in the eye. "If I had known, I would have told you."

"Why did you think that?" Ellie waved to the last people pulling out of the parking lot as they called out goodbyes to her and Josh. Dylan would probably hear that she had been hugging

Josh. But she wanted to get to the truth. "You keep telling me I deserve better, so start with giving me answers."

"Let's sit." Josh opened the passenger door for her and folded the roof of the jeep to let the breeze blow through. Hopping into the driver's seat, he faced her. "This summer, I noticed he quit hanging out with the group. We hadn't talked much after the play, so I didn't think about it much. Then, I saw him at Starbucks with that girl from the hospital. He was wearing his swim shorts, so I figured she was a lifeguard he worked with. Then, I saw them at Amazon Grill a few weeks later. Again, they weren't touching or acting like a couple, so I didn't know what to do."

"And you and I weren't talking, so you didn't want to bring it up to me." The pieces were coming together.

"You refused to talk to me, or so I thought, so what would you have done if I called and said I saw Dylan twice with another girl? He would have been able to explain it away or say I was making things up, and since you were still mad at me, you would have believed him." Josh gazed in her eyes. "Please believe me. I prayed and prayed that you would wake up and see what was happening because I knew he was a jerk but didn't know how to prove it. He's not the same as when we were younger."

"Well, walking into the hospital to find out he was with another girl was a wake-up call. I don't know what to think. He explained how it happened, and I see where he was coming from." Ellie filled him in on what happened the other night, including what Dylan said about the fight with Josh.

"Is that what he said?" Josh snorted. "That's one way to spin it."

"So tell me your side." Ellie checked her phone even though it hadn't rung. Had Dylan lied to her again?

"Well, a few days after I saw him for the second time, we ended up at the same party. The guys were talking locker room stuff, and someone called you the Ice Princess. It ticked me off, and I was even madder that Dylan laughed about it, like it was a joke that you still believed what we learned in Bible class or church." Josh pressed ignore on his phone.

"You can answer. You don't want to keep Lindsey waiting."

"This is more important. Besides I ignore most of her calls." He opened his call history, showing Ellie all the missed calls from Lindsey. She fought a smile. Lindsey knew Josh was talking to her. She was probably furious. "Well, I saw him go off to the side of the party a few times to talk on his phone, so I asked if he was talking to the girl I saw him with. He said I was just jealous that he had you and I didn't. I told him he was lucky to have you and was an idiot to jeopardize that. Then he sucker-punched me. I did hit him back though. Multiple times. And I won't lie. It felt good."

"I'm sorry that I caused your friendship to end." Ellie grabbed his hand. "Y'all were best friends, and it's my fault, I guess."

"Don't say that. He was the one hiding. He knew if we fought, he could blow off anything I said as me being jealous." Josh held on to her hand. His was warm and his palm rough. They reflected him, strong and stable.

"Why would you be jealous? That's ridiculous. You've never acted any way but as a big brother to me. And I appreciate it." A text came through her phone, breaking the moment.

"Hey, this is Cara. She's out with Mark but wants to spend the night. Let me reply." She typed a quick message saying she would be at home waiting for Cara to arrive.

"Can you believe my independent sister is dating someone?" Josh laughed. "My mom is thrilled. She's been waiting years for Cara to have a crush."

"I love it too. She's so cute getting nervous. It makes me remember when Dylan and I went on our first date. Even though we'd liked each other for a few years by then, I still had butterflies in my stomach." Ellie paused. "People think I should just walk away, but I feel like I'm walking away from more than just him. It's leaving behind my whole life's memories."

Josh took his time responding. "That's your choice, Ellie, but if you go back, you're missing out on the chance to make new memories with someone who won't cheat on you."

Scooping up her backpack, she jumped out of the car. "You offering, Josh?" *I shouldn't be flirting with Josh of all people.* Ellie blushed. "Thanks for the talk," she yelled as she ran to her own car before he could reply.

She started the engine and put it in drive. He had pulled up behind her and was waiting for her to pull out before him. He would be such a terrific catch for some girl. Just as long as it wasn't Lindsey.

The rest of the weekend was quiet. Ellie spent Saturday with her family, getting several promises of donations from businesses in the area for the missions trip, going to Nick's football game, and then spending the rest of the day putting out the fall decorations her mom insisted had to go up since it was nearly October. They finished the night with a movie marathon. Who would ever believe she would change from having a packed social schedule including romantic dates to sitting at home on a Saturday night?

Sunday, she missed church because she had to work at the last minute, covering for someone who came down with the flu. It had been years since she missed church but at least she wouldn't have to see anyone who might give her advice about her relationship with Dylan. After a few hours of helping customers and moving things around for the new merchandise that would come out next week, Ellie and her boss finally had a lull to chat.

"How are those college plans coming, Ellie?" Frances was an eccentric woman who loved fashion but didn't follow any trends, choosing what she liked and apologizing to no one for it. If only Ellie could be more like her.

Ellie froze, her back to her boss. "Still applying." She tried to sound casual.

"Well, time is flying by, girl, gotta get going. I guess you're still waiting on that boy to decide where he's going." Frances shook her head and went back to folding jeans, muttering about not understanding why a woman would let her life be dictated by a man's wishes. *Maybe that's why Frances is in her 50s and single.*

Ellie opened her mouth to respond but couldn't form the words. The door chimed, and Frances turned her attention to the women who walked in. What was she going to do? She had no plan. No career interests. Nothing without him. Ellie went to the bathroom to get control of herself, adjusting her happy mask for the world to see. Would it be easier to just go back to what she knew and loved than to be alone?

Ellie took extra care getting dressed Monday. Dylan would be back at school, and she wanted to look as cute as a school uniform would allow. When their shared pre-calculus class rolled around, Ellie smiled when he slid into the seat next to her.

"Hey, beautiful."

"Your face's better." Ellie busied herself opening up her book and notebook.

"Glad you noticed." Dylan laughed. As Mr. Thomas lectured, Dylan kept writing notes on his notebook and motioning for her to read them. *Forgive me. I love you. You're amazing.* He was wearing her down. How could she walk away from years of love over one mistake?

He hesitated before holding up the last note. *Hang out with me this week. We can hang out with a group if that makes it easier for you.*

For the first time, she replied with a shy smile. She wrote on her own notebook. *Xavier and Amanda maybe?* Her answer was rewarded with a grin that reached his eyes and melted her heart.

15

That night at dinner, Ellie told her family she needed to make an announcement. "I've decided to give Dylan a second chance." Silence. "Well, I told him we could hang out with a group. I'm not sure how I feel, but I can't walk away yet."

Her parents nodded but still didn't speak.

"I didn't know you were that stupid, Ellie." Nick shook his head.

"I know y'all may not agree with me, but I can't forget all the history we have. I love him, and I think our love is strong enough to move past this." Ellie twirled spaghetti around her fork but didn't take a bite.

"Relationships are hard, and your father and I will support your decision. You're almost an adult, and it's time you make your own decisions." Her mom patted Ellie's hand. Was she was speaking from the heart or spitting out a rehearsed answer? Her mom wanted her and Dylan to work things out, so of course she'd support this decision.

"We love you, Ellie, and we want what's best for you. I'm praying God makes the choice clear. But, ultimately, the decision is yours." Her dad went back to eating his spaghetti.

"I still think you're stupid." Nick dropped his fork on his plate and stood up, knocking his chair over in his rush.

"Nick, don't talk to your sister that way." Their dad's voice was firm.

"Well, I'm not going to sit here and pretend I think it's a good idea to take that loser back." Nick picked up his chair and took his dishes to the sink.

"I'm going to be careful, Nick. We'll hang out in groups and see what happens. I'm just open to the possibility it will work out."

"Whatever." Nick gave her one more incredulous look before going upstairs.

"He's just going through a tough age, and my health and your pain are just a little too much for him." Ellie's mom fidgeted in her seat.

"I am going to make someone mad no matter what I do. Friday night, I got basically the same speech from Josh."

Her dad took a long sip of iced tea before speaking. "Josh's a wise boy. I've always liked him. He loves Jesus and isn't ashamed of it. That's unique for boys his age."

"Well, he's not the one I love." She was going to have to defend her choice to a lot of people, and she was already tired of talking about it. Why couldn't everything go back to the way it was?

"And you don't have to love Josh, but when I pray for a husband for you, his love for Jesus is my first request." Now her dad wanted to talk, just when Ellie was finished.

"I get what you're saying, Dad, and believe me, I'm not rushing into anything." Ellie gave him a kiss on the cheek as she went to the kitchen and began loading the dishwasher, leaving her parents to discuss her announcement.

As she got ready for bed, heated voices were coming from behind her parents' closed bedroom door. Her father wasn't even trying to keep his voice down. "I don't know why you push her toward getting back together with that boy."

"I never told her to get back together with him, but I just want her to be happy. She was moping around, crying and depressed after they broke up." Her mom wasn't backing down either and was practically shouting for the first time in Ellie's life.

"And you think he'll make her happy? He broke her heart, and she's acting like nothing's wrong. You of all people know that's not healthy." Her dad's voice faded in and out.

Ellie's mom paused. "You're probably right, but like you said, she's almost an adult and can make her own decisions. I thought we both made that clear."

"Just don't push her toward him. I know you and Linda have your plans for a wedding, but our girl deserves someone better."

Now her mom was crying, but her dad comforted her with a soothing voice, asking her if she wanted to go sit outside on the porch and drink coffee.

Pushing her dad's doubts out of her mind, she climbed into bed, leaving her Bible on the bedside table and grabbing her phone instead. She sent Dylan a text. So, I told my parents we were going to hang out and see where things go. This wasn't the time to tell him no one seemed thrilled with the idea and that even she had some doubts.

I can't wait to see you. My parents were happy, and I am too. Dylan's reply came instantly. Ellie spent a few minutes standing up the picture frames that scattered the room. She would give the boy she loved one more chance, even if her dad didn't approve.

16

October was busy with football games, her mom starting chemo and radiation, organizing a group to participate in Houston's breast cancer awareness walk, and group dates with Dylan. Xavier and Amanda were their favorite double date partners, especially after a few awkward hours with Cara and her newly official boyfriend Mark. Cara had spent the night lobbing underhanded insults Dylan's way, and it had been two of the longest hours in Ellie's life.

Even after a month, Ellie declined solo dates. Despite their history, it was a little weird being around Dylan. It was a full time job analyzing every comment he made, worrying every time he didn't immediately reply to a text, and wondering where he was all the time. But, then he'd hold her in his arms as they lay on the trampoline in her backyard, and everything was back to normal.

The one downside was that Josh barely spoke to her. After she told him her decision, his mouth dropped open and he shook his head as if he couldn't believe what he was hearing. He still sat by her sometimes in English and left occasional cards in her locker, especially the first week of her mom's chemo and radiation, but it wasn't the same. She had chosen Dylan, and that somehow hurt him. There were rumors that he had gone on a couple dates with Lindsey.

With November came Dylan's 18th birthday. Ellie and Mrs. Linda spent two weeks planning a huge bash, inviting everyone in the senior class, plus all the cheerleaders and football players. His parents rented the back room of a popular restaurant downtown and hired a live band for dancing. Ellie told Dylan it would be their official first date as a couple again. It was going to be a special night.

She took extra care to straighten her hair, and she wore a beautiful strapless black dress that poofed out a little before hitting a few inches above her knee. Red heels and jewelry completed the ensemble. When Dylan picked her up, her mom took the standard pictures. Things might be returning to normal. Her dad wasn't around, just like he hadn't been around any time Dylan came to the house since they started dating again.

"You look amazing. I wish we could just go to the park, lie in our favorite spot, and make out." Dylan couldn't quit staring at her, and she had to snap her fingers and jokingly tell him to focus on the road several times before they pulled up to the restaurant. When they stopped, Dylan rested his hand on Ellie's thigh. "Before we go in, I want to do something." He unbuckled his seat belt, leaned over, and kissed her. Their first kiss since getting back together. She paused before returning his kiss, wrapping her arms around his neck.

As the kiss deepened, she pulled away. "We should get in. Let's continue that later." She was succeeding at playing hard to get. He jumped out to open her door, and they walked into the party with their fingers intertwined to the cheers of Happy Birthday. They were back on top of the world.

Soon only Dylan and Ellie remained as they said goodbye to all the guests. "I know it's my birthday, but I wanted to get you something." Dylan pulled something out of his pocket and handed it to her.

"You're so sweet." Ellie started to open the small Tiffany blue box, her heart racing.

"Before you open it, I need to say something." Dylan held her free hand and brought it up to his lips, kissing her fingers. "Those weeks without you were horrible. You've been the best part of my life. You're beautiful, and I'm lucky to have you." His eyes never left hers, and his hands ran up and down her arms. "I can't imagine life without you, and I wanted to show you how serious I am about that commitment."

"That's how I feel about you." She smiled and held up the box. "Can I open it now?"

"Yes." He rocked back and forth, waiting for her response.

She opened the box. Inside was a simple silver band with little diamonds that formed a heart in the middle. It was stunning. "It's beautiful, Dylan. I love it."

"Ellie, I promise to love you always, and one day, when we're older, I promise to put an engagement and then a wedding ring on that finger." He took the ring and slipped it on her finger, giving her one more kiss, a deep one that took her breath away.

"I love you, Dylan. I always have, and I always will." She ran her fingers through the hair that fell over his eyes.

"I know, and I won't take you for granted again." Holding hands, they walked to his car. He didn't let go even as he escorted her to the front door, and kissed her until the porch light flickered on and off several times, her parents' signal that it was time to come inside.

Lying on her back in bed, she couldn't quit staring at the ring on her left hand. It was beautiful. She took a picture of it to share with all her friends, but then didn't post it. It was a little more special when the promise was just between her and Dylan.

That night she dreamed of her future. She and Dylan were married with two kids, and she loved her life as homeroom mom and devoted wife. When she woke up, she glanced at her hand one more time. She was well on her way to achieving all her dreams. And those dreams all revolved around Dylan Grant.

17

Saturday promised to be a day of fun for Ellie and her mom. Although they usually started shopping on Black Friday, her mom had been worn out by the Thanksgiving festivities. As she dressed, Ellie gave thanks that chemo treatments would soon be over. The routines had been rough on the whole family. Her mom took her chemo on Thursday afternoons. The steroids included with the treatment kept her in high-energy mode for the rest of the day and all day Friday. But Saturday and Sunday were crash days, where she barely had the energy to get from her bed to the couch to spend time with family. Although this schedule was tough on family time, it was the easiest way for them to care for her without the kids missing school and her dad missing work.

On quiet Saturday mornings, Ellie and her mom caught up on TV shows. Then while her mom napped, Ellie cleaned house, and her dad and brother ran errands. Sundays were more of the same. She had missed youth group the last month because she was exhausted by Sunday night from caring for her mom and trying to do half of the things her mom did around the house in addition to schoolwork, cheerleading, an occasional shift at work, and mission trip planning.

Last Sunday, she had joked, "Well, it's good preparation for one day when I'm a stay-at-home mom like you."

"Taking care of you kids and your dad has been my life's joy." Her mom's voice cracked. Was it from the chemo, which often made her mom's emotions jump around, or just regular emotions? "Your dad saved me, and I will spend the rest of my life saying thanks."

What did that mean? She started to ask a question, but her mom was asleep. Ellie's mom had never talked about her life before she met Ellie's dad and joked that life didn't even start until she met him.

Ellie planned to ask her about it during their shopping trip. Her mom was in the middle of a two-week break from chemo, so maybe she would feel well enough. Ellie checked herself in the mirror one more time before heading out. Her jeans fit perfectly, and her green sweater made her brown eyes pop against her blonde hair that was pulled back into a loose braid with a few wisps hanging out for a casual effect.

"Mom," Ellie called out when the living room was empty. No answer. Her dad and Nick had gone out for a father-son breakfast before Nick's football game. Wandering into her parents' room, Ellie found her mom lying in bed, crying. Rushing to her side, Ellie started wiping her face with a towel that they kept near the bed.

"I'm so sorry, Ellie. I can't seem to get out of bed. I don't know why I feel so bad. I didn't have chemo this week, but I just have no energy." She could barely keep her eyes open.

"It's okay. I'll stay here by you. We can watch movies. Or, I'll watch movies while you rest." Ellie started to take her fuzzy brown boots off, but her mom stopped her.

"No, I've already called Linda to come over. I want you to go shopping, Ellie." Her mom reached out to touch her hand, and her hands were cold and a bit clammy.

"It won't be the same without you. I've been waiting to go with you. It's our day." Ellie couldn't keep her disappointment out of her voice.

"I feel horrible about it." Her mom tried to raise her head but crashed back down. "I've been wanting to do something normal, but here I am stuck in this bed, not even able to lift my head. I hate this. Just go! Quit arguing with me!" Her voice rose with emotion. Her mom rarely raised her voice, believing it unladylike, and Ellie gave up arguing.

Ellie's mom had never been like this. Her speech was always polished and her appearance spotless. Now she was forgetful, covered with rashes, and starting to lose her hair. Even though cancer attacked her mom's body, it drained her spirit as well, which was worse.

"I'm so sorry. I'm so sorry." Ellie kept repeating the phrase as she hugged her, putting her head on her mom's chest, careful of the chemo port.

"No, I'm the one who is sorry, Eleanor. You shouldn't have to see me like this. It's your senior year, and you're playing nurse."

"I just want to help you feel better." Ellie examined her mom's pale face for any sign she should stay. At least her eyes were open now, which signaled a little more energy. Maybe getting mad had been good for her spirits.

"I'll feel better if you go shopping. Call Cara or another friend and go to the mall. I'll give you my card, and I want you to start my Christmas shopping." Her mom pointed to her purse on the lounge chair near the bedroom window. "Go to the Galleria. I know you love it there."

True, it had everything from fancy stores where security guards watched the doors to an ice-skating rink. Not wanting her mom to be disappointed in her, she smiled.

"It won't be as much fun without you." Ellie bit her lip as soon as the words escaped. They would just make her mom feel bad for not being able to go.

"I know, but it will make me happy to know those gifts are being bought. You know our joke for your dad." Her mom gave a weak smile.

"We're not shopping, we're creating jobs for the fashion industry." Ellie had to laugh at their routine excuse when her dad calculated the total of their receipts from a day of shopping.

"Prop me up with some pillows, and then call your friends. Go create some jobs."

Ellie added pillows to get her mom closer to sitting up. She was already starting to fall asleep, so Ellie left the room to call her dad and give him a heads-up. He told her to go shopping, agreeing that it would make her mom happy to see all the stuff she bought as well as make less work for her mom when she did feel better. He and Nick were finishing breakfast and would come back home, skipping the game. Ellie told him that her mom was sleeping and Linda was on her way. He might as well spend time with Nick, who was still in a funk that he didn't want to talk about to anyone. Maybe a guy's day would help Nick open up. When she got off the phone, there was a quiet knock on the front door. She let in Linda, who gave Ellie a kiss on the cheek.

"You go spend some of your parents' money and let me take care of her." Linda's arms were loaded with Christmas card boxes. "I'm going to get my Christmas notes ready and then work on y'all's. I've got plenty to do, so you take your time."

"Yes, ma'am." Ellie grabbed her purse and headed out the door. She had been too focused on her mom to call any of her girlfriends. But if she couldn't be with her mom, she would be alone.

Finding a parking spot at the Galleria, Ellie pulled out the list of presents her mom wanted her to buy. Just tackling this list, not to mention her own, would take hours. Grabbing a coffee at the first shop she found, Ellie got started.

Two hours and a few hundred bucks later, she took a break to watch the ice-skaters. She had been to the rink countless times as a kid and a few times each year as she got older. Even though she wasn't a great skater, there was something fun about feeling the cool air flow through her hair as she glided across the ice.

Houston rarely got cold enough for even a tease of snow, much less an outside rink, so they created it indoors. For Christmas, there was a huge, beautiful tree with twinkling lights in the middle of the rink. One day she would go up North and skate on a real rink. Maybe if Dylan got a scholarship to one of the Midwest colleges he had talked about, it wouldn't be too long.

"Hi. Ellie, isn't it?"

Ellie turned to her left. Amelia. Why would she would say hi?

"That's me." Ellie forced a smile. "Christmas shopping?"

"Yeah, not having as much luck as you, I guess." Amelia pointed to the pile of bags on the ground that Ellie guarded with her legs.

"Working on my mom's list. She was too sick to come." Why was she sharing this with Amelia, the last person she wanted to confide in?

"How is she? Dylan told me about her, that night of the accident." Amelia seemed genuinely concerned.

"Not good. Chemo is supposed to help, but it seems it has just as many side effects as the cancer." Ellie looked back at the skaters. Vulnerability was the last thing she wanted Amelia to see.

"My aunt had cancer a few years ago. It's tough. I'm really sorry." Amelia leaned against the railing, watching the ice skaters too. "I feel so bad about what happened. I promise I didn't know. I thought he really liked me, but I guess he was playing us both."

"It's not your fault. Plus, we worked it out. See what he bought me." Ellie held out her left hand, watching Amelia's reaction to that bit of news. A single tear escaped Amelia's eye before she wiped it away and blinked the other tears away.

"Good for you." Her voice was now cold. "I knew I shouldn't come by and say anything." She turned to walk away.

Ellie put her hand down. "I shouldn't have said that. I didn't mean to hurt you. I can see you still care about him."

"I do. Or I did. I just wish I hadn't slept with him, you know? My mom always told me once you did that, you were connected, but I didn't believe her." Tears were streaming down her face now. "I can't believe I'm telling you this. I know he loves you and that he sees me as a mistake, but it's been hard getting over him."

Ellie edged back with each one of Amelia's words, tripping on her bags. She caught herself on the rink's railing.

Was she really hearing this? Dylan had told her he hadn't had sex with Amelia. He promised he was telling her the truth. Had he had been lying that night and every night since? Red flames rose up in her. Standing up, she struggled to control her breathing. She was smothering. She had to get out of there and into the fresh air.

"I've got to go. I'm sorry, Amelia. You deserve better. We both do." She gave Amelia a weak smile, picked up her bags, and started running. People stopped to watch the crazy girl with her arms full of bags. She knocked into people as she raced outside.

Outside, Ellie gasped for air as the tears poured down her face. Walking back and forth, she couldn't catch her breath. The people walking by blurred into one mass. Her hands shook too much to pull out her phone, and Ellie leaned against the wall, praying for God to help her breathe.

"Slow down. Take deep breaths." Appearing out of nowhere, a petite woman coached her. "In. Out. You're going to be okay."

Her face was vaguely familiar. Unable to place the woman, Ellie focused on the lady's kind face and steady words until she was able to take a deep breath.

"Is that you, Ellie Lansing?" The woman took Ellie's hands and squeezed them. "You've grown up since I was your Sunday school teacher."

When she had taken a few more deep breaths, she answered, "Miss Stacy. Wow, I can't believe it. I haven't seen you in years. I don't know what happened just now. It's been a rough day, and I guess I panicked."

Her chest tightened just thinking about what Amelia said.

"It's okay. Sounds like a panic attack. I'll stay with you until you're okay. Let's catch up." She led Ellie to a nearby bench and put her bags on the ground. "I saw you running, and the Lord nudged me to check on you even though I didn't recognize you at the time. I'm glad I listened."

Ellie spent the next twenty minutes pouring out her heart.

Stacy listened without interrupting until Ellie got it all out. "That's a lot to deal with, Ellie."

"I always thought that if I followed God's rules and did all the things my parents and youth pastor told me about, life would always be great. I know life isn't always perfect, but why does God let these hard things happen? I follow Him, so why am I hurting?"

"I don't know what He's trying to teach you through these situations or why you're going through so much, but I can pray for you. Can I cover you in prayer now?"

Ellie nodded and bent her head as Stacy prayed.

"My husband and I are youth pastors now. Here's our business card. You know, I hate malls and do most of my Christmas shopping online, but I felt a tug to come here today. I'm so glad I did. Jesus loves you, Ellie, and the fact we ran into each other proves it. Please call me and let me know how you and your mom are doing."

"Thank you. I'll stay in touch." Ellie walked to her car. Jesus loved her. She had known that all her life, and she believed He sent Stacy to help her. He probably even sent Amelia so that Ellie would learn the truth. But that didn't change the fact that her life was still a complete mess.

She took off Dylan's ring and threw it in the back seat. Her stomach clenched. She had to bury her anger before she went home. *This is the last thing my mom needs.*

She took the long way home, stopping at the water wall downtown. Families picnicked on the nearby grass, and couples posed in front of the 64-foot tall fountain. People scurried around, smiling and laughing. But she sat in silence on the steps, watching the water rush down the wall.

As it grew dark, she headed home, practicing a smile convincing enough to fool her family. She was surprised to find the garage and house empty. She checked her phone and found four missed calls from her dad.

"Darn it."

She could barely get through the first message. "Sweetheart, we're at the hospital. Your mom's battling an infection. The chemo has compromised her immune system. It's serious. Please call." Ellie had read that a low white-cell count meant simple illnesses often took a turn for the worse, fast.

"I can't believe I left her here." Ellie spoke to the empty house. Her dad called while she was deleting his messages and throwing the presents into her mom's closet.

"Ellie. Hey, sweetheart." Her dad sounded tired.

"I'm so sorry I wasn't there, Dad. I let her down."

"It's okay. She told you to go shopping. I told you to go shopping, too."

"I need to come see her. I'm on my way." Tears choked her.

"Please, don't drive upset, that's just as dangerous as driving drunk. Just stay there. Cara or Dylan can bring you. Call one of them." Her dad's rare no-nonsense tone suggested the gravity of her mom's situation. Good thing he wouldn't know how mad she was just an hour ago while driving.

"Okay. I'll text Cara now." Ellie hung up and called Cara. She didn't answer. She was probably out with Mark. Dylan would be the last person she would call, so she tried a few girls from the cheer squad. No answer. What good was it to have a ton of friends if none of them answered their phones? She started pacing as she scrolled through her contact list. She stopped at Cara's home number. Mr. or Mrs. Martin would take her to the hospital without a second thought.

She pressed call and waited while the phone began to ring. Someone answered on the fourth ring.

"Hello."

Josh. Just perfect. "Hi, it's Ellie. Is your mom or dad there?"

"No, do you want me to leave a message?" His voice was cold.

"No, forget it." Next to Dylan, Josh was the last person she wanted to help her.

"Ellie, why would you call my parents? It must be something." The edge was gone. Now he was more like the guy who left her note cards with verses and drawings.

"Well, my mom is in the hospital, and my dad won't let me drive there upset. But no one is answering their phones to take me, which is making me even more upset." Her voice rose with each word as her frantic pacing threatened to wear out the kitchen throw rug.

"I'm on my way."

"You don't have to. I can call a cab." But he'.

Ellie went outside and paced up and down the driveway as she waited, peering down the street every few seconds for a sight of Josh's black jeep and checking her phone for a call or text from her dad. She sent her dad a text saying Josh was bringing her to the hospital.

There was a new text from Dylan, who had heard about her mom. He offered to come up to the hospital, but she replied that she was fine. He was out fishing with Xavier at a lake in the suburbs, a good hour's drive away. Good thing Dylan wasn't in town, or he would insist on coming. She couldn't deal with him right now. After months of lying to her, he deserved a few lies back, so she told him the hospital wasn't allowing any nonfamily visitors. Dylan replied that he loved her and would be praying for her mom. Ellie didn't respond.

After the longest ten minutes of her life, Josh's jeep pulled into her driveway, and he jumped out to open the door for her. She climbed in and leaned back against the headrest.

"Thanks, Josh. Knight in shining armor once again." Ellie tried to smile when he climbed back into his seat, but her lips barely moved.

"My cape's in the back seat. Seriously, your mom's going to be okay."

"I hope so." Why was he at home on a Saturday night when everyone else was out having fun? Probably drawing or painting. With things weird again between them, she couldn't ask. Instead, she reached over to turn on the radio. Maybe it would drown out her thoughts.

"I see the ring is gone." He glanced at her as he pulled to a stop sign at the exit to her neighborhood.

"Yeah." She gave him a 'don't ask' glare, and he didn't press. Was that a smile on his face? He looked to the left and she couldn't quite tell. After a few minutes, the cheerful Christmas music got on her nerves, and she clicked the radio off. "Not in the mood for all that."

He laughed at her wrinkled face, and she shot him another glare. "Sorry. You know my rule about the driver controlling the radio, but there you are flipping it on and off like you're in charge."

"Shut up, Joshua." The words came out harsher than she meant them.

"Lansing, I know you're in a bad mood and your mom is sick, but you can't just treat me like a punching bag when you need to get your feelings out and then ignore me when life goes back to perfect." He gripped the steering wheel with both hands and peeled out of a red light, tires squealing.

"Like you ignored me for months after the play? I didn't ask you to pick me up. I'm sorry I'm not perfect." Ellie turned back on the radio, flipping the volume as loud as it would go until Josh covered her hand with his. She moved hers, and he clicked the radio off.

"I never asked you to be anything but yourself. That's enough for me, but you know what? Get it all out. Let me have it." His jaw was clenched.

"I just want to scream," she whispered.

"Then scream." Josh rolled down the windows, and Ellie gave a weak scream. Josh didn't even look at her; instead he turned on the radio. She let out a louder scream. He increased the volume again. She screamed once more, so hard and so long she gagged. When she grew quiet, he rolled the windows back up and clicked the radio off. "Feel better?"

"You wouldn't believe. My mom once watched this talk show where the counselor told people to go to a forest and scream to let go of their anger. We laughed that it was a little too weird, but I guess it works." Ellie stared out of the window. "I'm just scared she's going to...."

Josh didn't say a word. He just took her hand and held it in his strong grasp until they pulled up to the hospital.

"Thanks. More than you know, thank you." Ellie hopped out and ran through the automatic doors, searching for the elevator that would take her to the fifth floor. While she waited for the elevator to arrive, Josh sprinted through the hospital doors and bent over next to her, out of breath. "If football doesn't work out, consider track."

"Found a close parking spot and then sprinted in. Want company?" He was still out of breath. Just how close had that spot really been?

"Don't you have plans on a Saturday night? Won't Lindsey be waiting for you?" The doors opened, and she jabbed the number five several times.

"You know, you bring her up a lot. You jealous or something?" He pressed the 'door close' button and leaned against the wall.

Ellie blushed. Josh was the kind who would never cheat on his girlfriend. He was constant and true. *Why does Lindsey have what I don't? She doesn't deserve a great guy with the way she treats people.*

"For what it's worth, we broke up. Well, if you can call three dates a relationship. When you need a laugh, ask me about that."

"I could use a laugh, but here we are." Ellie slid through the doors as soon as she would fit and flew down the hall with Josh right behind her.

18

"How's Mom?" Ellie wrapped her arms around her dad, who met her at the door.

"She's sick, baby. Real sick." He kept his arm around her, guiding her to the bedside. Her mom's face was so washed out it almost matched the white pillow. Her thin hair was wet and matted against her head, and she didn't have on one of her stylish wigs purchased the day her hair started falling out in clumps in the shower or when she brushed it.

Ellie's mom was connected to several machines and had IVs running medicine to her ailing body. "The doctors say she caught a cold, but it's turning into pneumonia fast. They're giving her antibiotics and steroids, but you know her immune system is compromised."

"I shouldn't have left her. I'm so sorry, Mom." Ellie caressed her mom's hand and gave her a kiss on the cheek.

"It's not your fault, Ellie." Nick stood next to her with puffy red eyes. He was too young to watch his mom suffer like this. Their dad put his arms around them both.

"She's a tough one. Putting on that happy face no matter what's going on around her has made her one of the strongest people I've ever met."

Ellie's dad turned to Josh, who was standing outside the door. "Come on in, Josh. Thanks for bringing Ellie. I didn't want her driving upset. You're a good friend." He patted Ellie's shoulder and walked over to Josh, shaking his hand before embracing him.

"It was no big deal. I'm happy to help. I'll leave y'all alone, but please call me if you need anything." Josh glanced at her dad and Nick, but he lingered when he looked at Ellie.

"I'll walk you out." Ellie walked to the door and matched his step down the hall. "I'm sorry for treating you like a punching bag. You didn't deserve that."

"When it's you doing the punching, I don't mind, lightweight."

Ellie laughed. He was always teasing her about her size. When they were about 13, he overheard her whining about being so short that no guy would ever kiss her because she would need a ladder to reach his lips. For the next year, he would ask her if she needed a ladder every time he saw her. She had grown a few inches since then, but he still liked to tease her. "It's like I'm on a roller coaster of emotion. You must think I'm crazy. Screaming earlier, crying in the room, and now laughing."

Josh stopped at the elevator and reached out like he was going to hug her but settled for an arm pat. "I don't think you're crazy. I think you're finally letting out your bottled-up emotions. That's a good thing." He gave her a smile as the doors opened. "Call or text me if you need anything. Anything at all. I'm your personal punching bag." He rubbed his abs. "I can take it."

She thanked him again and waved as the doors shut. She stopped by the vending machine for coffee. They were going to need the caffeine to make it through the night.

19

They needed caffeine for more than just a night. Ellie's dad didn't leave his wife's bedside until Thursday night when her fever broke, a sign the infection was receding. Even then, it was just long enough to go home to get a better shower and grab his work laptop. Both of her parents were exhausted by the time they got home Friday night: him from staying up most of the night to watch her sleep and her from the intensity of the illness.

Ellie's dad carried her mom into the house. She laughed weakly, reminding him how he carried her over the threshold of their first apartment after their honeymoon almost twenty years before.

Would a guy ever love her like her dad did her mom? Not Dylan. She could define it now, what real love was. It was holding someone's hair back while she puked, telling her how beautiful she was when she hadn't showered in days because she couldn't even hold her head up, and praying over her when she slept. Whatever she and Dylan had, it wouldn't ever be as true as what her parents had demonstrated this week.

Not able to deal with her mom's health plus Dylan's excuses plus people's gossip and pity, Ellie had dug up the silver promise ring in the back of her car where it was wedged between a floor mat and a balled-up t-shirt. Putting it on was like tying herself up with one of those chains used for prisoners, but she had to make it through the week. So, she put on her best smile when she saw him, ducked his kisses, and used caring for her mom as an excuse to avoid hanging out.

In English class, Josh pointed at the ring. She shrugged and shook her head, but he didn't let it go.

"What's up with the ring?"

Mrs. Hensley had asked them to turn to a neighbor and discuss the theme of Hawthorne's *The Scarlet Letter*, too much of a coincidence for Ellie, who cringed every time the teacher talked about Hester's scarlet *A* for adultery. Ellie twisted the ring. Maybe she could throw the ring in the trash and escape the classroom and the topic that hit close to home—cheating. "Too much to talk about now. I just couldn't deal with him and my mom."

"Does he know? Want me to beat him up again?"

Josh had been so good to her, so she tried to reward him with a smile, feeble as it was. "As I recall, he gave as good as he got."

He flexed his muscles. "I've been working out. Seriously, what's up?"

"It's okay. He lied to me about what happened with Amelia." She filled him in on the facts while Josh filled in the answers on the worksheet. His jaw clenched when she repeated Amelia's words about what made her the saddest.

"That idiot. Who does he think he is? Stupid." Josh fumed until the teacher stopped by and asked him if he was okay. "Yes, Mrs. Hensley, just can't believe Hester had to suffer alone while the guy got off scot free."

She smiled and patted him on the back. "Good cover, Josh, but get back to work."

"Close call. Here let me write some stuff. We want her to see both handwritings." Ellie took his pen, pulling away as their hands brushed.

"He's just like this creep Dimmesdale in the book. You get ridiculed while he enjoys his popularity. What an idiot!" Ellie let him vent. After all, he was saying all the things she wanted to but couldn't yet.

At home Friday afternoon, she took the ring off and put it on the nightstand. She looked at her bare hand. She was going to have to live without her crutch. Her whole life had revolved around Dylan. What would happen next? She might not know herself without him, but she couldn't delay any more. Amelia's confession had changed everything.

First thing Saturday morning, she asked Dylan to meet her at the park. He had morning workout plans but promised to be there after lunch. Getting dressed in jeans, a white lace shirt, and a pink button-down pea coat, she practiced her break-up speech in the mirror. Her hands shook as she paced underneath "their" tree, where they had carved their initials in the bark when they were sixteen. The place he had first told her he loved her seemed fitting for the end. The tree was bare in the semi-cold southern winter, but its strong trunk and sturdy branches whispered that she too could survive the emotional winter to come.

His car pulled up, and she took a deep breath, preparing for what she wanted, no needed, to say. The end. After months of pretending things could go back to normal. His shaggy hair that she used to think was sexy was no longer attractive. His blue eyes were shallow, and his grin no longer enticed her. In fact, her stomach churned as he pulled up the hoodie on his gray jacket.

"What's up?" He leaned in for a kiss, but she moved away. "What's your deal? You've been treating me like dirt all week. You don't return my texts, won't kiss me, and blow me off every time I try to talk to you. Then I see you all chatty with Martin, and I heard he drove you to the hospital after you told me only family was allowed. You replacing me with that chump?" His eyes turned stormy.

Strengthened by his selfish words, she was ready to let him have it. But her rehearsed speech evaporated.

"Are you kidding me?"

"No, I'm not kidding you. I have jumped through every single hoop you've thrown out there, trying to prove how much I love you, and you still can't get over what happened." He stood there with his arms crossed and a frustrated expression on his face. Every time they fought, he somehow managed to make everything her fault. Not this time.

"Kinda like you treated Amelia?" She met his gaze, watching for a lie.

"What are you talking about? I told you I broke up with her, and you check my phone every day, so you know I don't talk to her." He kicked a rock and took a step back.

Ellie took a step forward. "Yeah, you slept with her and then dumped her."

"Where did you hear that? You know people make up stuff." His fallen face told her everything she needed to know.

The grief in Amelia's eyes had been real, a reflection of Ellie's own pain. No way she made it up. Ellie tucked her hands in her pockets and whispered, "She did. I ran into her at the mall."

"So that's why you've been avoiding me. I'm sorry you found out that way." He walked toward her with his arms out. "I didn't want to tell you what I did because I didn't want to hurt you any more than I already had."

Ellie took the ring from her pocket and held it out to him. He made fists with his hands, and crossed his arms.

"You were so upset, and your mom was so sick. I didn't want to disappoint you when you asked. I didn't think you really wanted to know the truth." He walked closer until his chest bumped into her outreached arm.

"The lies need to stop, Dylan." Ellie kept holding the ring out. "You thought I wouldn't find out since Amelia doesn't go to our school or know anyone we know. But, the truth always comes out eventually. Why couldn't you just tell the truth?"

"If you want the truth no matter what it is, here it is." Dylan met her gaze, and Ellie flinched at his hard stare. "After so many years of dating, you still wouldn't have sex with me, so I found someone who would. How's that for the truth?"

Ellie gripped the ring tighter and brought her hand to her side. Her hands shook as he continued. "Connor was right. You are the ice princess. Hot to look at but cold to the touch. Don't you know you're the locker room joke?"

"Just shut up, Dylan." Her voice shook, but she held back her tears. He'd never see her cry over him again. Unable to think of something more to say, she threw the ring. It hit the tree's trunk and fell to the ground.

"No, you sit there, doing everything your parents or the church tells you, and you never live. You built up our relationship to this amazing love story like the stupid romance novels you read, but the truth is, every guy wants sex, Ellie. So, be prepared to be dumped again when you don't give it up." His eyes were a stormy sea, like the Nantucket bay during the worst storm of the summer.

He picked up the ring and shook his head. "One more thing." He stopped and looked at her before continuing. "I didn't mean to hurt you, Ellie, but we might as well face the facts. We were trapped, and I wanted out. If I have to be the bad guy, that's fine. I felt bad your mom was sick, and I didn't want to hurt you. You wanted the truth. And that's the truth."

Ellie backed up, leaning against the tree for support. In all the years she had known Dylan, she had never seen him so hateful. He could be snobby and a little condescending to other people, but never to her. "So why did you try to win me back? Why not walk away?"

"My parents threatened to make me quit football if I didn't 'do the right thing,' and I thought we could finish the school year hanging out. I still want a football scholarship. I couldn't believe they would threaten my college plans. But they said my relationship with you was more important with football. We had a huge fight about it. They insisted they were dead serious. So, keeping things the same made it easier to at least get through high school. Once we got to college, it would be easier to break up. Now I can say you dumped me. But everyone at school will know what's going on. Look at yourself. Your life's not so perfect anymore, is it?" He turned his back on her and stalked to his car, not even giving her another glance before his tires screeched his exit.

Ellie sank to the ground, gasping for air. The same sort of panic attack she had at the mall threatened to smother her, but this time, there was no one around. She tried to cry out to Jesus through her tears, but there was no release. Her phone vibrated against her leg, and she pulled it out. A group text from Connor, inviting everyone in the senior class to a party at his house that night since his parents had decided to go to the A&M game a couple hours away. He promised a fun, parent-free night, which meant alcohol and hook-ups.

I'll show them I'm no ice princess. She sent Cara a text, asking if she was going, but Cara replied that she and Mark were going to the Rockets game. At least she wouldn't have to talk about what happened. Although her best friend knew she was going to break up with Dylan, Ellie wasn't ready to tell her how Dylan had responded.

Ellie walked the paths in the park, trying to gain control of her emotions. She could deal with her rage later, but there was no way she was bringing her sadness into the house. The doctor had encouraged them to stay close as a family, telling them that positive thinking and a will to get better were often just as important as medicine. She would wait until her mom was stronger to tell them what was going on. Tonight would be about forgetting. Forgetting Dylan, the plans she had, and the good girl reputation that got her nothing but pain.

Driving home, she cranked up her music. She touched up her make-up and smoothed her wild curls as best she could before going inside. All the years of practicing the 'perfect daughter' face served her well. Her parents were watching a movie, and Nick was at a friend's house for some much-needed fun. When she asked if she could go to the party, her parents agreed without questions, trusting their obedient daughter. "Just remember to lock up and turn on the alarm." *I'll set some alarms all right.*

Giving them both a kiss on the cheek, she didn't stick around. Even though they both seemed like they could fall asleep any minute, it wouldn't take them long to see she wasn't herself. Upstairs, she took down every picture that included Dylan and dropped them in the trashcan. Every gift, stuffed animal, or other trinket he had given her she pitched into a trash bag. She ran the memories to the garbage can outside the garage.

Getting rid of the reminders was the first step, but back in her room, the holes where Dylan had been were everywhere. Her bookcase and dresser top were nearly empty, and all but one of her photo frames now displayed the paper picture that came with the frame. Her room reflected her heart. Empty. She stared at the one picture left, the drawing Josh had given her. She hugged the wood frame to her heart and did her best to stifle the cries that tried to escape.

She blasted some Carrie Underwood to cover the noise as she cried into her pillow. She lay on her back and stared at her closet. Focusing on her outfit for the night was easier than thinking about the rest of her life alone. She searched through her wardrobe. Dylan was right. She was an ice princess who wore clothes that fit a 30-year-old, not a seventeen-year-old cheerleader. She found her shortest dress, one she had bought but forgotten to return. Not her usual style, the teal lace dress clung to her body but didn't cross the slutty line. Pairing darker make-up with chunky jewelry and stilettos, she stared at her reflection in the mirror. Her darker look matched her mood. Spraying on perfume and grabbing a black coat, she was ready to go prove Dylan wrong.

She struggled to catch her breath as she pulled out of the driveway. What would people say? She should go back in her room and start making plans for her future. What school would she go to? What career was she even interested in? No. Too many questions waited back in her room. Taking a deep breath, she headed toward Connor's house on the next street. The driveway was lined with cars. Dylan's car was one of them. Good. Let him see her.

Connor opened the door and took a step back. "Wow! Let me take your coat, Princess Ellie."

"Isn't it Ice Princess, Connor?" Ellie took off her jacket. His gaze trailed up and back down her body.

"Not tonight, I can see. What was Dylan thinking?" Connor whistled.

"Who cares?" She pushed out a fake laugh and gave him a long hug.

"That's right, forget about him. He's dumber than I thought for breaking up with you." Connor put his arm around her waist and led her into the party.

Ellie started to correct him. But he would end the night so drunk that he wouldn't remember what she said anyway. All of her classmates stared when she entered the room. Some must be shocked the good girl was here when parents weren't, and a few were probably a little unsure of what to think about her outfit.

Most of her friends from church would leave in an hour or two when the drinking and hook-ups started. A few football players looked away, and she followed their gaze to Dylan. His eyes were locked on her. His jaw dropped a little. She gave him a wink on her way to the kitchen to get a Coke.

As she wrote her name on her cup with a Sharpie, a few girls were already gossiping about her. She leaned against the door leading back to the party. How was Dylan spinning their breakup?

"I can't believe she's here." The first voice was Lindsey, which meant Melissa's voice should be next.

On cue, Melissa said, "I know, and looking trashy." Ellie winced. Melissa was the reasonable one.

"Do you think Dylan thinks she's still hot?" Perhaps Lindsey had set her sights on Dylan now, forgetting Josh. Typical.

"Nah, he asked you to come here. He's been flirting with you all week, and now we know it's because he dumped her."

All week. Melissa's words were a swift kick in the gut, and Ellie held onto the countertop, cooling her nerves on its cold granite.

She shouldn't do it, but she turned the corner and confronted the two girls who had pretended to be her friends for years. "I broke up with him, Lindsey. Today, in fact. So, he wasn't single when he was flirting with you. I'd watch out if I were you."

"That's not what he's saying." Lindsey flipped her hair as if that would swat Ellie away like a fly.

"Well, it's the truth. And if you're here as his date, you should know that he expects you to sleep with him, and if you don't feel ready, be prepared for him to get it elsewhere. That's what he did to me. Don't let him lie to you." Ellie's eyes softened. Although Lindsey was a jealous snob, she didn't deserve to fall for Dylan's lines.

"He said you had already moved on to Josh, and he busted you with him." Melissa cut in the conversation since Lindsey's mouth was still hanging open. "I had no idea he did that to you. We all know he cheated on you, but you forgave him and then were always with Josh. His explanation made sense."

"You can't believe everything you hear, just like I can't believe y'all spend so much time gossiping about me without ever coming and asking me the truth. You've cheered with me every day for years, but I guess you don't know me at all." Ellie stalked away before they could say anything.

Finding an empty loveseat, she sat down to people-watch, hopefully shrinking into the crowd. Telling off Lindsey and Melissa had drained her. *What was I thinking? I don't belong here.* The crowd started dispersing as the kids who had an early curfew left and the beer came out.

I'm here because I will not let Dylan, or Josh, or anyone else, define who I am.

When Connor came by with drinks, Ellie accepted a beer, and when Dylan put his arms around Lindsey as they danced, she took a long sip. It was gross, even nastier than she felt, but when his lips met Lindsey's, she kept drinking, no longer noticing the taste.

Her gaze met Dylan's, and she held eye contact as she pulled Connor onto the loveseat and kissed him. He returned her kiss. When they broke apart, he said, "Yeah, definitely just a princess. Nothing icy about that." He pulled her up to dance, and she let him wrap his arms around her and draw her close. She had never had anything more than a sip of wine before, so halfway into the second beer, she was buzzed. Dylan looked her way before pulling Lindsey in for a kiss, and Ellie downed the rest in one gulp and started on the third one that Connor held out for her.

After the third beer, the room began to spin, and she leaned on Connor for support. He took that as encouragement and kissed her again, moving her toward the edge of the dancing crowd. She closed her eyes and let him lead her, not wanting to see people watching her, not wanting to see who she was kissing, not wanting to see herself in the wall mirrors. He asked her if she wanted to go upstairs. When she didn't answer, he pressed her into the wall, kissing her deeply.

As her head bumped the wall, she came to her senses for a moment. Josh was walking into the living room. He hadn't seen her yet, but his gaze darted around the room. He approached Dylan and spoke animatedly. Connor was now kissing her neck, her body stuck in his embrace. *Josh, turn around already!*

Dylan shrugged, and Josh shook his head and turned to another group of people, who pointed her way just as Connor started to lead her up the stairs toward his room. She followed like a zombie.

"Back off, Connor. Can't you tell she's half drunk? She can't even walk straight." Josh jerked Connor around and pulled his arm off Ellie.

"No, you back off, Josh. She's a big girl, and she decided to have a beer. She's also the one who kissed me first. She picked me, not you." Connor gave Josh a shove and tugged Ellie up a few more steps.

Josh barged between them. "Do you want to go up there with him?" His eyes pleaded with her not to go.

Ellie couldn't form the words, but she shook her head no. Josh reached out, and she fell into his embrace.

"Man, I wouldn't have forced her into anything. She wanted it." Connor tried to defend himself to the growing crowd.

Ellie laid her head on Josh's shoulder as he guided her down the stairs. Melissa met them at the door with Ellie's coat. "I'm sorry, Ellie. I should have stood up for you." A deep red flush crept across Ellie's face, but she kept walking. *I've made a fool of myself.*

Josh didn't say a word as he put her in the passenger seat of his jeep and leaned over her to buckle her up. He drove out of the neighborhood onto the freeway. Ellie stared out the window at the fuzzy scenery that flew by. *Do not throw up.*

After a few minutes, he handed her a bottle of water, and she took a few sips before putting the bottle down. Her stomach churned, and the car seemed to be spinning. How did people do this all the time and call it fun?

"Here you are rescuing me again. You should start charging a fee. Where are we going?" He was heading in the opposite direction of their houses.

"I'm not ready to talk yet, Ellie. Just drink the water." Josh handed her the bottle of water again. Ellie fell asleep against the jeep door. She woke up about thirty minutes later as he pulled into a fast food restaurant. Finally, the spinning stopped.

"Do you think you can walk to the bathroom? I'm going to get you some fries or something." His voice was tense. Why didn't he just drop her off at home if he was so upset?

"That would be good." She unbuckled her seat belt and let him guide her to the bathroom.

"Wait here for me when you finish." Josh headed over to the counter to order. He was already sitting at the table nearest the bathroom when she came out, eating fries. "I was about to go in and get you."

"I was splashing some water on my face." Ellie ducked her head and slid into a chair, resting her head on the table.

"Let's go." His gruff tone pulled her out of her seat. She grabbed his arm while they walked back to the jeep in silence.

They exited the freeway and were heading to the suburbs. "Can you tell me now where we're going? Are we by the airport?"

"Yeah, we're going to watch the planes come in. I can't bring you home like this." Josh pulled onto a side road near the airport landing strip. A few cars were there. It was a popular place for dates, but Dylan had never taken her there.

He opened the roof of his jeep and offered her a blanket, but she shook her head. The cold breeze stung as it awakened her. They leaned back in their seats in silence. Josh ate his burger. Ellie ate a few French fries.

Finally, Ellie whispered, "How did you know to come?"

"Melissa felt bad about y'all's conversation and called me. She thought you might do something stupid to get Dylan's attention." Josh continued to watch the plane coming in, its lights blinking against the black night.

"I'm glad she called. I owe her. And you." Ellie looked at him, but he kept his stare frozen on the sky. "Are you mad at me?"

"Yes. I don't even want to think about what would have happened if I hadn't shown up. Would you have slept with him?" He finally met her gaze. She was shivering, and he tossed the blanket on her lap.

She forced herself to look into his eyes. They were cloudy with emotion. "I don't know. I just wanted to feel something different. Dylan called me all kinds of stuff today." Ellie focused on the blanket. "I just didn't want to be myself."

"Why do you care what he says?" Ellie cringed at his harsh tone.

"I've loved him forever, Josh, and when the guy who holds your heart tells you that you mean nothing and that since you didn't have sex with him he had to get it somewhere else, it hurts like... like..." Ellie sat up. "Do you know what it's like to love someone so much and realize you mean nothing to them?"

Josh still lay back in his seat, staring at her. He reached up and tucked strands of hair behind her ear. "I do, Lansing. I've never been in a long relationship like you have, but I know how it is to watch someone you love with someone else."

She leaned back into her seat. Who on earth was he talking about? "Surely not Lindsey. Maybe Sydney. I heard y'all dated this summer. I didn't know it was serious though."

"It wasn't." They sat in silence for the next hour, watching planes fly in.

"Why did you pick this place?" She hadn't dared to look at him. Had he fallen asleep?

"I've been out here before with my dad, and you get a picture of how small you are when you see those huge planes fly in, carrying hundreds of people to and from Houston."

I'm already small. So small God doesn't even see what a wreck my life is, or if He does, it's too little of a problem for Him to worry about.

Josh continued, his voice passionate. "See the sky, Lansing? It's huge. You're amazing, but you're focused on our little private school bubble. But there's a big world out there waiting for you. Opportunities you never dreamed about because you were so focused on being Mrs. Grant one day."

He grabbed her hand and pointed her finger to the stars that filled the sky. "That's you. Life is dark, but you're going to keep shining. You can't see how bright you are in your dark situation, but if you step outside of the pain, you would see what I see."

"What do you see? I just see sadness." She brought their hands down but didn't let go.

"A girl who lights up a room when she smiles. A girl who takes care of a sick mom instead of going out and having fun. A girl who stood up for my sister when the rest of her 'friends' teased her for saying she was saving her first kiss for her wedding day." He laced his fingers with hers and turned to her. "A girl who is the most beautiful person, both inside and out, I have ever seen."

She smiled. Would she ever see herself like he did? "You just feel sorry for me, Josh. You've always been a softy. Remember the worms?" Back in middle school, she, Cara, and Josh had been at the swimming pool. When Josh walked to the edge to do a cannonball, he almost stepped on a worm baking on the cement in the Houston heat. She and Cara watched him dig a little hole in the grass and put the worm back in the soil. They had told him he would be a paramedic or firefighter with his need to save everything. He had been doing that for her the last few months, putting her back in the soil when she was dying in the heat.

"I feel a lot of things for you, Lansing, but sorry isn't one." He gazed back to the sky, covering up a yawn with his hand.

Ellie watched him. He wasn't gorgeous like Dylan, but he was handsome in a rugged way. His crooked smile was the only thing that stood out in a crowd. But there was something special about him. He yawned for a second time. "We should go before you fall asleep on me. My parents are going to freak."

He brought his seat back up and put the canvas covering back on the jeep. "I sent them a message that you were going to crash with Cara. My parents know though."

"They're going to think horrible things about me." Ellie dug in her jacket pocket for her phone. "I'm so embarrassed."

"They love you, Ellie. It's going to be fine." Josh patted her arm and began the trip back home. He found the local Christian station and kept the Christmas music playing low, which lulled her back to sleep. What seemed an instant later, he was shaking her.

"We're home." He jumped out and ran around to open her door.

"Why is my car here?" She blinked, trying to wake herself up.

"Nick gave Cara your spare key. They brought the car here so that no one would get the idea you spent the night at Connor's house." He reached out and let her grab on to his arm to steady herself. How would she explain this to Nick tomorrow morning?

"I can't thank you enough." Ellie stopped before he opened the front door.

"No need." He leaned against the door, holding his key next to the lock, waiting for her to finish.

"Yes, I need to tell you how much..." The door opening interrupted Ellie's thoughts. Cara rushed out to grab her arm.

"I can't believe I was at a game when you needed me." Cara gave her a hug. "You're going to be okay, Ellie."

"I know. Josh helped me see that." Ellie turned to him. "He's been my knight in shining armor." Josh answered with a shrug and squeezed her hand before Cara whisked Ellie into the bedroom where she dropped onto the bed and fell asleep.

The next morning, Ellie woke up early with a headache. When she stretched her arms, she found a piece of paper next to her pillow. *Take a shower and feel free to raid my closet. I'm having breakfast out with Mark before church. Love ya!* Ellie ran through the events from the night before. Drinking. Check. Embarrassing herself in front of her cheating ex-boyfriend who was already with someone else. Check. Getting rescued by the brooding but super sweet guy who was always there. Check. Last night had all the makings of a TV movie, so why wasn't she happy at the end?

She got up. There was a second note propped up on the dresser. *Thought you might need these.* Next to it was a bottle of ibuprofen and a bottle of water. She swallowed a couple of pills, praying they worked quickly. After a long shower, she took the sheets on Cara's bed, which now smelled like a night of stupid choices, to the washer. Holding the huge bundle of quilt, blanket, sheets, and pillowcases in her arms, she ran into a wall.

"Dang, Lansing. You trying out for linebacker? You almost knocked me over." Josh reached down and picked up the linens that had fallen to the ground. Ellie stared at his arms that held her last night and now took her load again. When she tore her gaze away, she met eyes that burned into hers, seeing straight to her soul. She was speechless. What do you say to the guy who keeps picking up your pieces, literally and emotionally? She mumbled a weak thanks.

"How are you feeling?" He dumped the sheets in the washer and grabbed the remaining items she carried.

"Better. I still don't have the right words to tell you how grateful I am for what you did last night." He didn't glance at her as he added the detergent to the machine and pressed a few buttons. "I can't imagine what would have happened if you hadn't shown up." Ellie touched his arm. His muscles tensed under her fingers. "Please look at me. I was a mess after my fight with Dylan, and who knows what stupid thing I could have done."

"Well, thank God you didn't find out. Let it go. I don't want to think of you going up those stairs with Connor." He shoved his hands in the pockets of his jeans and walked away.

"Are you still mad at me?" He had shown such sweetness last night, but now he was cold.

"A little." He didn't glance her way as she followed him to the living room.

"I know I made a few dumb mistakes last night, but I didn't ask you to rescue me." *Ouch, that didn't come out right.* "I'm so glad you did, but I guess I just don't get why you were so kind last night and distant this morning." She wrapped herself in a throw quilt Mrs. Martin had sewn and sat down on the couch.

"I feel like my parents did after I wrecked their car back when I was fifteen and went joy riding. They were so concerned when they met me at the hospital, but as soon as I was okay, the anger came out and I was grounded for three months." Josh sat down next to her.

"I see. So, I'm the kid, and you're the parent. What are you going to ground me from?"

"I would ground you from thinking about Dylan if I could." Josh shook his finger at her and imitated an old man's voice, "I hope you learned your lesson last night."

Ellie smiled. "I hope so, but I think the hard lesson is just beginning."

"Maybe, but remember you have people who are here for you. People who love you." He faltered on the last two words. Did he include himself in the group that loved her?

"I love them too." No matter who he meant, she wanted him to know she loved him. He was a true friend, and if it hadn't been for him, she might have woken up in Connor's bed this morning.

"You're so beautiful. Inside and out." He touched her cheek with his fingers, and Ellie's skin sizzled under his touch. His eyes searched hers, and she leaned toward Josh and closed her eyes, waiting for his kiss. Instead of feeling his lips on hers, his hands cupped her chin, and the he gave her the softest brush of lips against her forehead.

Heat flooding her face, Ellie pulled away from his embrace and stood up. "I'm so sorry. I don't know what I'm thinking." Josh leaned back into the couch while Ellie ran into Cara's room to gather her purse. What was she thinking? She had just thrown herself at the one guy who had been a true friend. She fumbled around for her phone and keys.

She raced to the front door, but he blocked her way. "Sit with me on the front porch swing." She tried pushing past him, but he grabbed her arm. "Trust me," he whispered as he opened the door and let her go through.

She opened her car door and then paused. He was sitting on the swing, waiting for her. She joined him on the swing, focusing on the trees, their leaves dropping with each gust of wind. Their bare limbs swayed but didn't break. Josh didn't speak.

She leaned her head back and the rising rays warmed her. "Too bad Houston can't be like this all the time, 50s and sunny."

"I guess I should get to the point. Do you remember when you asked me about the play, and we were interrupted before I could explain?"

"Yeah, but what does that have to do with how I made a fool of myself again this morning?"

"I was excited to be in the play with you. We had always been friends because of someone else. Think about it. When we hung out, it was because I was tagging along with you and Cara or because Dylan was around."

"True."

"I had a blast getting to know you without them around. When you were with Dylan, it was always about him, but when you took the leading role, you were the star instead of standing in his shadow." Under that spotlight, doing something different and being someone different had been fantastic.

Until he had stood her up in front of hundreds of people.

Why couldn't he just tell her why he walked away? "I felt that way too. You were so funny, and I loved goofing off with you."

"Seeing that side of you, I began to have feelings for you, more than just friendship." He propped one leg on the swing, and faced her.

Ellie jerked her head toward him, her mouth falling open. Dylan said Josh had a crush on her during the play, but hadn't

Dylan just said that to cover his own lie? "I had no idea. You're making that up to make me feel better."

"Dylan knew, and he called me out on it. You were so wrapped up in him, you didn't notice me." Josh was silent for a few minutes.

Running a mental marathon, Ellie searched her memories. Josh had never acted as if he had feelings for her. He was his normal goofy self. "So, if you had feelings for me, why didn't you kiss me when the play called for it?"

"I froze. Here was this gorgeous girl that I had known for years but had just realized was awesome. You were beautiful, and you were looking up at me like you were in love with me. I knew you were just acting, but I meant the feelings behind the words."

"You froze." She had thought of hundreds of reasons he had walked off the stage, but having feelings for her never crossed her mind.

"I did. I had wanted to kiss you for weeks, but it was more than just acting for me." Josh leaned forward and touched her arm. "I know this is the worst time to tell you that, but kissing you a few minutes ago would have been a mistake because I've wanted to kiss you for almost year now. And, I don't want our first kiss to be pretending in a play or a way to forget the hurt you feel. I want it to mean something."

"I'm not sure what to say." Ellie could hardly breathe and her arm felt hot under his touch. She leaned next to him, her shoulder fitting perfectly under his arm.

"I know you don't feel the same way, and that's why I haven't told you. We were just getting back to being friends, and I didn't want you to feel pressured or uncomfortable."

"I don't. Just confused." Ellie surveyed his face, just inches from hers.

"Well, when I saw the hurt in your eyes earlier, I knew I had to tell you that every time I see you, I want to kiss you, but you're worth the wait for it to be the perfect timing." He leaned back, releasing her from his hug, and held her hands, kissing her palm.

"Worth the wait, huh? I don't know if anyone has ever described me as that." It reminded her of something her dad would say.

"That's the phrase I hear in my heart and my head every time I pray, asking God for you to wake up and see me, really see me." Josh let her hands go and looked up at the squirrels scampering from tree to tree.

"You prayed for me?"

"Every day, and always got the same response. 'She's worth the wait.' So, I've waited, and I'll keep waiting until you're ready." Josh stood and reached for her hand.

Ellie put her hands in his and let him pull her up and into a hug.

"I know I keep saying it, but you're an amazing friend. More than words can express." Ellie emphasized the word friend and smiled her first real smile since she ran into Amelia. A smile that reached down into her heart and gave her hope. "I should get home, and you need to go to church. I have a lot to tell my parents. Tell Cara thanks and I'll catch up with her later."

"You got it, Lansing. Now, don't let what I said go to your head." He tapped her nose.

"No, but I'm letting it go to my heart, Joshua." She drove away, watching him in her rearview mirror. He stood there, solid, until she pulled onto the next street.

At home, the first thing she did was ask her parents if she could skip church. Of course, they wanted to know why, so Ellie filled them in on the weekend's events, starting with what she learned from Amelia to the breakup with Dylan to her conversation with Josh Saturday afternoon. Her parents had always told her she could tell them anything, but she had never tested their tolerance until today. She ducked her head when she was finished, her cheeks hot.

"I could kill that boy." Her dad's face was nearly purple, but he wrapped his arms around her and held on tightly. "I'm just so thankful you're okay."

"I can't believe it. I just can't believe that Dylan would come into our home and pretend to be a part of our family when he had done that. I wonder if Linda and Robert know. They should know what a jerk their precious baby is." Of course her mom went straight to what this looked like instead of focusing on how Ellie felt.

"Don't be mad at them. No matter what he does, he's their kid. They didn't know he cheated on me, so I bet they're in the dark about how far it went too." It was hard enough getting over a broken heart and the embarrassment of being so naïve about her boyfriend without having to discuss it with her parents. *At least I didn't have sex with him.*

"When we calm down, we should talk to them." Her dad was always the voice of reason. "Dylan is an adult, but his parents should know what he's doing so that they can make sure he's aware of the consequences." He gave Ellie a kiss on her head. "I'm just glad you didn't fall for his lines, baby girl. Your mom and I are proud of you."

"Thanks, Dad. That does make me feel a little better, but I have a long way to go. It's only been a day, but I feel like I'm not myself without him. I thought maybe if I tried another church, I could make a fresh start. Learn who I am on my own."

"Who you are is just fine." Her mom went back to scrambling eggs.

Ellie rolled her eyes and looked to her dad, the mediator. "Maybe you could contact Stacy. Didn't you mention her husband is a youth pastor?"

"Yeah, it was a total God thing that she was there when I needed someone, and I liked her a lot. I'll go find her card." Ellie dashed to her room. *Hopefully it's not too late.*

The butterflies in her stomach fluttered as she entered the church alone an hour later. When Stacy greeted her inside the door with a hug and an introduction to a few girls, Ellie took a slow, deep breath. She didn't know anyone here. Perfect.

After a sermon on what it meant to be a Good Samaritan in today's world and a time of prayer and singing, the teens moved to a room upstairs. A band played a few songs before Stacy's husband Micah taught a lesson. Ellie sat in the back, content to observe, but a group of girls invited her to their small group for prayer. Although Ellie loved her family's church, it was a release to be with strangers where she was just Ellie, not Dylan's girlfriend. Ellie, the girl who was going through a rough time, not the always-perky cheerleader or responsible daughter.

Maybe this is the place to meet myself.

The Sunday high was followed by a Monday crash. Would kids still be discussing why she and Dylan broke up and whose fault it was? Would they be passing around pictures or gossiping about her partying? Would she have any friends left?

Even though he hadn't won homecoming king, Dylan was still a popular guy as the star quarterback. The football team would take his side, pulling along a lot of the cheerleaders and other jocks. How was she going to make it until June? *Why am I even thinking this way? This isn't about taking sides.*

This was the last week of football—the championship game, and then one more week until Christmas break. She could do anything for ten days.

"Did you do something stupid again last night? You look horrible." Nick had covered for her Saturday night, but he seemed more disappointed in her than her parents had.

"Thanks, Nick. You know how to make a girl feel good." Why couldn't he drive so that she could put on a little more make-up before school?

"Just preparing you for how people are going to treat you." Nick gave her a sly smile. "If you can make it through me, you can take on anyone. I do it for you."

"I will seek my revenge. Just wait." Ellie hit him on the head as he darted past her to get in the car. It was good he was tough on her. If she practiced on him, she would be ready for whatever people had to give.

Her resolve lasted less time than it took her to walk through the front doors. Whispers greeted her.

I heard she almost slept with Connor.

I heard she was cheating on Dylan with Josh.

I knew she wasn't as perfect as she wanted everyone to believe.

Ellie ducked into the bathroom and hid in a stall, trying not to cry, not to give anyone the satisfaction of seeing that they got to her. For four years, she had gone out of her way to always smile, to always say hi, and to be nice to everyone, and this is how they returned the favor? Coming out of the stall, she clenched the sink, staring into the mirror and taking deep breaths. Her make-up couldn't cover her washed-out complexion and the dark circles under her eyes. She sank to the floor between the sinks and buried her face in her hands.

Cara walked into the bathroom, calling for her. "Ellie, are you in here?"

"Yeah, down here." Cara reached out her hands and pulled Ellie up. "Did you hear what they're saying about me? He cheated on me, lied to me about it, and even slept with someone while promising to love me forever, but I'm the bad one?"

"Relax. You're better than that. Remember when we tried out for cheerleading and we dealt with the dumb cheerleader jokes? You were the one who said to ignore the words and prove them wrong with our actions. So, you go out there and prove them wrong." Cara pointed to Ellie's reflection in the mirror.

Ellie smiled at Cara's swinging arms and loud voice. "You should consider a career in coaching. You'd have that team ready for victory." She hugged her friend. "Seriously, you're right, and I'm so thankful for you. Walk out with me?"

Cara walked Ellie to each class, guarding her from the curious stares that lined the hallway, but she couldn't protect Ellie in pre-calculus, where she had to face Dylan. He was already sitting with a group of friends when she tried to sneak in at the last minute. Instead of avoiding her eyes, he seemed to seek her out. Instead of ignoring her, he laughed as his friends made fun of her drunken state on Friday night. Instead of respecting their past, he bragged about what a good kisser Lindsey was. The substitute teacher was oblivious to it all, and the guys got bolder with every joke.

The more the guys talked, the closer the walls came. Her chest tightened, and her stomach rolled. Ellie closed her eyes and counted her breaths like Stacy had taught her, but they got shorter and shorter until she was gasping for air.

Sweat dripped down her back. Ellie fanned herself with her notebook, but it didn't stop the room from becoming smaller and hotter. Standing up, she snatched her purse and ran out, her lungs begging for fresh air.

The school secretary stood up as Ellie darted past the front office, but she ran to the bleachers and stood in the cold air until her heart rate returned to normal. She couldn't go back in there. She couldn't face them. She couldn't be the punch line of a joke from the guy who had claimed to love her for so long. She walked around the football field. There would be no Stacy or Josh this time. She would have to get through this on her own, so for the first time ever, she skipped school.

She slid into her car, rolled the windows down, and drove, following the freeway until it ended at the bridge onto Galveston Island. Although it wasn't beautiful Nantucket, it was water. The Gulf was too cold to get in and a little too brown for her to even want to, so she walked to the end of the pier and hung her feet off the edge. She matched her breathing to the cadence of the waves coming in and the tide pulling back.

Eventually, she pulled out her phone. Twenty calls and texts waited for her. Her heart raced, so she put the phone down. She couldn't deal with anyone, no matter how well intended their thoughts were. She flipped to her stomach and let her tears roll but she didn't take her eyes off the waves. Their hypnotic motion kept her breathing steady.

Going to private school all her life, Ellie had prayed in front of people for years. But as she sat on the pier, alone with her hurt, the words stayed buried in her heart. Stacy had said that God was big enough to handle her anger and strong enough to handle her hurt. *We'll see if she's right.*

"God. Why? I did everything right, and my life still sucks. What is the point of making good choices if my mom will still get cancer and my boyfriend will cheat and lie? I can't breathe, I'm hurting so much." Ellie stood up as she hurled question after question at the One who created the waves in the ocean and those in her own heart. When she lost her voice, she leaned back against the railing on the side of the pier and just listened and watched.

The waves still rolled in and out. The sea gulls still scampered around for food. A few people still lingered along the beach. Nothing changed physically, but inside, Ellie there was a sweet, quiet response. *Choose me. Not rules. Not People. Me.* The words resonated in her spirit as she sat on the pier in silence for the next half hour.

"I don't know if I even know how to do that, but I'm willing to try." Behind her, the sun began to set, casting soft shades of pink and orange across the water. She marveled that the One who made the scene in front of her loved her for who she was, not what she pretended to be. The sudden winter darkness brought Ellie back to reality. She checked her phone again. 25 messages. Most were from people fishing for the gossip by pretending to be concerned.

She texted Cara that she was okay and sent another to her angry cheer coach that she was sorry for missing practice. Skipping practice might result in being benched in the last performance of the football season, but that didn't seem important any more.

As she drove back, she called her parents. Her dad answered on the first ring. "Ellie, where are you? What's going on?"

"I don't want to talk about it yet, but I'm okay. I'm coming home."

He didn't press. "We were worried when we got a call from the school secretary. I'm glad you're okay. We'll talk when you get home."

After a long lecture from her parents and a promise not to skip school again until senior skip day, Ellie went to her room, where she pulled out her Bible and searched for the story about Jesus calming the seas for the scared disciples. She read His words in red until she fell into an emotionally spent but peaceful sleep.

21

Friday night was perfect Texas weather for high school playoff football — clear skies and a cold wind. Fans bundled up in jackets, and the cheerleaders wore tights under their skirts. The players jumped up and down in place to keep their muscles warm. After giving Ellie a tongue-lashing, the coach allowed her to cheer her in what might be her last football game.

Lindsey and Dylan chatted by the bench while the team warmed up and the cheerleaders hung signs. *Maybe Coach should have benched me. That would have been easier than watching those two flirt.* Although the rest of the week had been much the same as Monday, Ellie had managed to get through each day by holding on to the experience on the pier. But having to stand here while Dylan and Lindsey flirted was gut wrenching. *I must be a glutton for punishment.* Then Josh walked up, blocking her view of the lovebirds.

"Lansing, it's our last game. Are you going out with a bang?" He did a cartwheel and waved his arms around, making her and the other cheerleaders milling around laugh.

"If you mean just trying to survive the night with a bang, then you got it." She kicked her leg up like they were performing a routine.

"Don't let him keep you from enjoying the night. You love to cheer, and I love football. I'm not letting him ruin my last game." Josh blew on his hands to warm them up.

"I guess the rumors have been rough on you too."

"I take it as a compliment when they say I'm the reason y'all broke up. You know part of him is mad that people say I stole you from him, but I guess the truth would be more damaging to his golden boy rep." He ran his hand across her cheeks, stung by the wind. "Cold?"

"Not so much." His touch quickened her heartbeat.

"It's going to be a great game. Did I tell you I got accepted to SBU's early admission? They can't offer me a football scholarship until later in the year, but I'm confident I'll get one." Josh's face lit up.

"That's awesome, Josh. I'm proud of you."

"Yeah, it will be cool to be a part of a new program and still be close to home. You should apply there." He gave her a quick wink. "You know Cara wants you there."

Ellie hadn't even thought about college since she and Dylan broke up. She had sent applications to all the schools Dylan was looking at, but now she wouldn't follow him across the street, much less 1,000 miles away. She had also applied to a few places near Nantucket, where her aunt lived. She hadn't heard anything yet, but choosing a college was now one more thing she would have to do on her own.

Snapping out of her daydream, she said, "I'm sorry. Got lost thinking about college. I haven't heard back from any. I guess I should start worrying."

"My mom's always told me this—when God says no to one thing, it's so He can say yes to something better."

Was he talking about colleges or something more?

"I've never thought of life like that before. Your mom's awesome." Ellie bounced on her toes, trying to stay warm.

"You're more than welcome to come by tomorrow to tell her." He took off his sweatshirt and offered it to her.

"You inviting me over?" Ellie tried to flirt but got her head stuck as she put his warm shirt over her cheer uniform. It was huge since it had to cover his football pads, and it fell below her skirt.

"I might be there with something to show you. You know, if you want to come talk to my mom." He pointed to the stands and waved to his mom, who waved her pom-poms.

"Then I might be there. Around two." Ellie gestured at the football coach, who was calling for the guys to start going through warm-up drills. "Good luck."

"That's what I have you for." Josh teased as he ran to the group.

Although it was an intense game, the Eagles lost in the closing seconds. Instead of cheering for Dylan, she watched the crowd. Little girls with cheer uniforms imitated their moves, and the teen boys scrambled to catch the t-shirts the squad threw into the stands. Cheering had always been about encouraging Dylan and being a part of him, but for tonight, it was about interacting with fans, supporting her school, and perhaps yelling a little louder when number 12, Joshua Martin, scored the only touchdown for the Eagles. Although the game brought the season and Ellie's football cheering days to an end, it seemed God was saying yes to a new beginning.

The next morning, Ellie woke up before her alarm went off. Since the breakup with Dylan, she seemed to be on the outside looking in. Her so-called friends had quit talking about her within hearing distance, but they didn't call to hang out. Even Amanda, who was more her friend than Dylan's, had seemed uncomfortable the one time they went to the mall together. It was probably because Xavier and Dylan were so close. Cara and Josh were her only two true friends, and since Cara was in a new relationship, she was busy a lot. Although she invited Ellie along often, Ellie didn't want to be a third wheel like Cara and others had been with her and Dylan over the years.

Stacy promised her things would go back to normal as she found a new routine, but did she even want normal anymore, especially if normal meant fake?

The sun was shining, and Ellie was going to enjoy the day even if it hurt. Not knowing what Josh had planned, she dressed casually in jeans and a t-shirt. She put Josh's sweatshirt over it just in case they were going outside. She spun around in front of the mirror, checking her reflection from every angle. All this effort for hanging out with a friend?

Driving over to Josh's house, she thought back to her conversation with her mom a few nights ago. Her dad and Nick had gone to a Texans' game, so she and her mom were indulging in a girls' night. Manicures, pedicures, facial masks, and chick flicks with hot chocolate and popcorn. Halfway through the movie, when the meant-to-be couple was realizing their feelings for each other, her mom paused the movie.

"Ellie, I've been thinking about something."

"What's up?" Ellie sat up in her recliner. It had to be important for her mom to turn off a movie at the best part.

"Well, when you told us about what happened last weekend, you mentioned Josh always rescuing you and that he said he had feelings for you." She paused. Since she started treatment, she loved to use "chemo brain" as a playful excuse for when she mixed up or forgot things. Even though it was often funny, it was hard on her mother not to have the exact right words to say.

"Yeah." Ellie smiled. The movie's actor had nothing on Josh.

"I've been praying about that. You know I have to start letting you make your own decisions, especially now that you're almost eighteen. You've always been such a responsible girl, and your dad and I are proud of the woman you are becoming. I just don't want you to rush into anything."

"I'm not rushing into anything. He said I was worth the wait, and I really don't know how I feel. I'm still in shock about Dylan to be honest." Ellie curled up under the throw blanket.

"That's what I mean. You're hurt, and when you're used to having a boyfriend, it can be hard to learn to be by yourself. Josh is a wonderful boy, and I'm thankful he's been a friend for you. But, I don't want either of you to get hurt."

"So, what you're trying to say is that he cares for me more than I care for him, and you don't want me to break his heart."

Caught, her mom laughed. "Pretty much. I also wouldn't want you to miss out on a great guy because you rushed things. He's pretty special. He reminds me of your dad."

Ellie picked up the photo of her parents on their wedding day that stood on the end table by her recliner. "What do you mean? You told me Dad saved you, but you never said why."

Her mom sighed. "Growing up, my mom dated guy after guy after my father left. She was determined that each man was 'the one' and that if she was perfect, he would love her forever. She changed herself—from her hair color to her hobbies to her likes and dislikes—depending on whatever the man liked. I was in the way, but since she was stuck with me, she told me I had to be the perfect daughter so that I wouldn't annoy her future husband."

Ellie moved next to her mom on the couch and put her arm around her. "I never knew. You seemed to get along with Grandma."

Returning the embrace, Ellie's mom continued, "Well, she had her first heart attack when you were just seven, so she didn't have the health to keep chasing men. From the time I was six until I went to college, I tried to be perfect to make her happy, but it was never enough. Each day she would tell me what I did wrong. Sometimes it was that I was too pretty and the man looked at me too much. Other times it was that I didn't clean up the apartment enough. Each time the guy left, it was my fault. Thankfully, I got a full scholarship to college, and I escaped."

"Mom, I'm so sorry. That must have been hard."

"Your dad sat next to me in freshman English class. He needed a pen, and of course, I had five lying in a perfectly straight line. He teased me about it, and for the rest of the semester, he sat next to me and borrowed a pen."

"That's why you still buy him pens for his birthday."

"Yes, it's our little joke, but he saved me from myself, Ellie. By the end of the year, he had almost all my pens because he never returned them or my heart."

"Aww." Ellie smiled as her mom blushed.

"It wasn't always easy, Ellie. I used to wake up an hour before him for the first year of our marriage because I didn't want him to see me without make-up. Not because I thought I was ugly but because I thought you had to look perfect to keep your man happy. I cleaned the house top to bottom every day so that he wouldn't come home to a messy house."

"Man, I thought you were bad now. I'm glad I didn't have to help you clean every day!"

"You're what changed me, my sweet girl. Giving birth was too painful to worry about make-up, and once I saw your sweet face, I didn't want to be that way anymore. I finally grasped Jesus' love for me when I saw how you loved and needed me. I know I still have a long way to go; it's hard to break the cycle. When I see you putting on your happy face when you know you want to be in your jammies crying it out, I see myself, and I'm ashamed that I taught you that being perfect on the outside is more important than dealing with the inside."

"I'm tired of trying to be perfect." Ellie took a sip of hot chocolate. She didn't blame her mom for her problems, but how should she phrase it?

"Well, cancer has taught me a lot of things, especially that night in the hospital when I couldn't even wear my wigs." Her mom was quiet for a minute.

"I was so exposed—out there for everyone to see my flaws. But, there your dad was, loving me as much as the day he married me, if not more." She patted Ellie's hand. "I was so wrong, Ellie. I pushed you onto Dylan and convinced you that you had to be my definition of perfect instead of who God created you to be. I know Josh cares about you, but you can't rely on him to fulfill your every need. I want you to be a strong woman who finds herself in Jesus alone. Then you'll be ready to love a man with your whole heart, not just a piece of it."

"I don't even know how to heal. I just go in circles. Feeling a little better one day and not being able to breathe from the hurt the next."

"Although you're free to follow your heart, I think it would be good if you made a decision not to date for a while. Learn who you are on your own." Her mom sighed. "Did that come off as telling you what to do? I promised your dad I wouldn't interfere, and I'm not. I promise. I just wish I had taught you this years ago, but I'm still learning it myself."

"Then how can Dylan find 'love' the next day with Lindsey while I can't get through the day without at least one cry-fest?"

"It's how God made us, and I promise you that Dylan is dealing with this in his own way, but his way is not healthy and will catch up with him." Her mom reached out and tucked Ellie's hair behind her ear. "My mom cycled for years, never dealing with my dad walking out. If you don't deal with your feelings, they will eat you alive. It's taken me years to deal with my past."

Ellie ate a few bites of popcorn. "That just sucks because it feels like our relationship meant nothing to him. When will I get to the point of not caring?"

"I don't know, but as long as you feel that way, your heart isn't ready for a new relationship."

"You're right, Mom, and I guess it makes me respect Josh even more that he hasn't pushed anything. Most guys are like Connor, ready to take advantage of a broken heart looking for a rebound guy." Ellie grabbed the remote. "Let's finish the movie. I'm not sure our couple will make it."

Pulling into the Martins' driveway, Ellie repeated, "We're just friends. He doesn't expect more." Before she could even ring the doorbell, Josh opened the door.

"Are you ready?" His eyes sparkled, and his grin matched hers.

"You're smiling like you did that time you asked me and Cara if we wanted to try the cookies you made and then recorded our reactions as we took a bite and realized their main ingredient was salt."

"I've grown up, Lansing. I can't believe you don't trust me." He cast her a hurt puppy look as she pushed past him into the house, greeting his parents, who were remodeling their office.

"It was last year, Josh." Ellie called back as she gave his mom a bear hug.

Holding Ellie tight, his mom whispered in her ear, "I'm sorry you're hurting, and you're welcome here any time, no matter which one of my babies you're here to see."

As she pulled back from the hug, she whispered back, "You know I feel at home here."

"Y'all plotting against me? I promise I don't have any cookies. I just have something to show you. Let's go." Josh motioned for her to hurry up.

"He's been getting ready for this all morning, so I guess we'll have to catch up later. Will you stay for dinner tonight? Mark and Cara will be here, and we're going to have a family night."

"Sounds per—" Ellie almost said perfect, but she was going to break the cycle of expecting and craving perfection. "Sounds fun." Giving the Martins a wave, she headed out to the garage with Josh.

"This is amazing, Josh." A temporary art studio filled the garage. Music pumped, old sheets covered the floor, and a small bookcase full of different paints stood between two easels that held blank canvases. "Are you going to paint two at once? I didn't know you were *that* talented."

He handed her a brush. "No, you're going to paint one."

"I'm not sure I have the talent for an actual canvas. Maybe I should start with a sheet of paper."

"No, because I know what you'll do. You'll get all your emotions out on the paper and then paint a pretty little flower or smiley face on the canvas, thinking that's what you should display. I want you to put your emotion on that canvas. All of it." He handed her one of his old Texans' t-shirts. She took off his sweatshirt and slipped on the t-shirt. His scent clung to every fiber of the soft cotton. *Maybe his shirt will transfer some talent.*

"So, what do I paint?" Maybe some waves like the ones on Nantucket. Those would be easy.

"Whatever you're feeling. You've been through a lot. Your mom's health. Golden boy. Me telling you how I felt."

"That would be the flower part of the drawing," Ellie joked. What if she put her anger and hurt there for anyone to see?

"You can draw that next. For now, just get your feelings out with the paint. I'm going to try something new—just picking colors and moving the brush. I always have a picture in my mind when I draw or paint, so I'm going to just go with the flow, not thinking about it too much." He faced his own canvas and examined the paint for a minute before picking up his brush to mix a few colors together.

He was giving her privacy, but she couldn't pick a color. Instead she watched as he moved the brush to create bold stokes covering the entire canvas. Every time she started to dip her brush in the paint, she checked to see if he was watching her. But he was absorbed in his own work and oblivious to hers. She began to paint happy yellow swirls. *At least it's not a smiling sun.* She started experimenting with mixing colors and even dabbing blobs to give a little texture to the painting.

She looked over to Josh, who was focused on his painting. Occasionally, he would stand back and analyze his work, but he didn't say a word or glance her way. She finally let the floodgates open, and out rushed a frenzy of paint. Over her carefully painted swirls and globs of "texture," she began to just splatter the paint. Colors slid down the canvas, leaving streaks of mixed color before hitting the floor where they met her tears. When she finished an hour later, there was a mess of color: swirls mixed with lines, light contrasting dark. A confused mess that mirrored her own feelings.

She stepped back.

"It's beautiful." Josh's words broke her concentration.

"It's a disaster. I can't tell what it is other than paint." Ellie crossed her arms. Oh no, she had gotten paint splatter all over his shirt, the ground, and all over her arms. Even her shoes were speckled with paint. "Sorry about the shirt."

"Don't change the subject. Your painting is real, and that's what makes it amazing."

"I guess you're seeing something I don't."

"What I see doesn't matter. What do you see?"

"I see the perfect swirls covered up with a mess." He wouldn't judge her, right? "I guess it's how I worked so hard to keep up the appearance of perfection, and now all this other stuff just came and threw up all over my happy swirls." She stepped to her painting and looked closer. "I do feel better though."

"That's how I feel when I draw, and I had hoped it would help you have a positive way to deal with your feelings." He picked up his paintbrushes, putting them in a jar full of water.

"Better than anger management classes. Thanks, Josh. This was fun, the most fun I've had in a long time. I would hug you, but I don't want to get you all painty." She handed him her brushes, and he took her hand.

"I don't mind a little paint." He brought his arms around her, and they just stood there with her head on his chest and his cheek on her head. His heart beat faster. Her mom had advised her not to jump into anything, so she pulled away and turned her attention to his painting, a beautiful display of splashes of green and blue.

"Now that's good. Can you explain it, Mr. Fancy Artist?" Ellie pretended one of the clean paintbrushes was a microphone.

"Yes, thanks for asking. I'm calling it 'Hope'." His eyes twinkled. He was talking about her, or maybe them. "We'll put these over to the side and then you can take yours home when it dries."

"I don't know if I want to claim that mess." She picked up the paint near her easel and looked at her painting.

"One day it will be a reminder of what you went through." Josh stood behind her. "And I think you'll see God make something beautiful out of what you thought was a mess."

"That's what I'm hoping for. I just don't see it most days." Ellie moved her painting off to dry and picked up the sheets off the floor.

As they walked back into the house, he offered to take her paint-covered shirt. Ellie burst out laughing while he blushed. "I didn't mean it like that. I meant to wash it. You have another shirt under there, you know."

"Stop, you're making it worse." Ellie was still laughing. If only her hands weren't full so she could snap a picture of the usual jokester as red as a tomato and stumbling over his words. "I know what you meant, but you should see your face."

Josh darted into the kitchen to rinse the paintbrushes while Ellie took the paint to the craft room. After putting away the supplies, she took off his shirt and put it by her purse, wanting to keep it to remember this day. It would make the perfect sleeping shirt since her old ones from Dylan were now decaying in the landfill, right where they belonged.

Christmas vacation couldn't come fast enough. A two-week break followed by the ten-day senior mission trip. The last fundraiser was a huge garage sale held during the school day, allowing students to purchase new and gently used items for Christmas presents. Ellie and the rest of the planning committee spent most of the day out of class, pricing and organizing materials. Area stores had added merchandise to what the seniors had donated. Wading through the junk that was going to the trash, Ellie shook her head at what some people donated…used socks, broken cell phones, and clothes with stains on them.

"I think people just cleaned out their cars and dropped their stuff off." Cara held up a used toothbrush. "No wonder everyone else went for lunch. To avoid this."

"I know. Who thought these were a good idea?" Ellie crinkled her nose as she threw away another pair of old flip-flops.

"The last three classes have done a garage sale and done well. We still need money to buy supplies for the trip." Cara held up a pretty silver picture frame. "Look, sometimes we get stuff like this."

"That is pretty. Wait, that's mine." Ellie grabbed the frame and stared at it. "I bought this for Dylan with a picture from our first official date. What bag did you get this out of?"

Cara pointed to the bag next to her, and they emptied the mementos: frames, hats, t-shirts, and a few necklaces. All things she had given Dylan throughout the years and a few things she had left at his house, like her pink scarf. "Why did he donate all this? Surely he knew I was the one collecting the donations."

Ellie sat on the table, holding one of the necklaces in her hand. Cara sat down next to her. "He's a jerk, Ellie. I didn't think guys were cruel like that, but I guess he is. There's one more thing." She opened her hand and showed Ellie a ring. The promise ring Dylan had given her at his birthday party, when he swore to love her forever.

She took the ring. The band was still shiny, and the tiny diamonds sparkled. The night he had given it to her had been one of the best nights of her life—full of hope and promise. "Would it be wrong to pocket this? Technically it was mine."

Ellie tried to smile but couldn't. Their relationship was truly over, piled into a brown paper bag. A lifetime of memories tossed away like they never happened. She had thrown away her old memories of him. Of course he would do the same. But turning them in to the garage sale fundraiser? Could he be any more hateful?

Putting the ring down, she ran her fingers across the photo frame. Which picture had been in it? Even though she and Dylan had liked each other since the day the cooties wore off, her parents wouldn't let them go on dates alone until she was sixteen. For their first solo date the week after Dylan got his driver's license, they had both dressed up and gone out to eat at a fancy steakhouse in Houston. It was the night they shared their first kiss. She had printed out the pictures the next morning and framed the best one in a silver frame that said 'forever,' which turned out to be just a few short years.

No tears came. Just regret for spending so many years focused on a boy who wasn't the one. Cara gave her a hug and began to organize things into piles. "I'll buy this stuff and then put it where it belongs. The trash."

"Thank you. That means a lot to me." It would be horrible if someone in the school bought the items that held her memories, but the school should still get some money for it.

After school, she drove to the neighborhood park. She and Dylan had hung out at the park countless times as kids, creating their own little world on the jungle gym. He was always the one to save her from the bad guys. Next to the playground was a small pond where people fed the ducks. Sitting on a bench in the gazebo, she took the ring out of her pocket. Cara hadn't noticed that Ellie took it and left a few dollars.

The ring she once thought was beautiful was now marred by broken promises and regret. Praying for healing, she stood to throw the ring into the pond, wanting to watch it sink under the murky water. The ducks, trained to look for food thrown at them, swam over. She couldn't let one of them choke on the ring. The last thing she needed was guilt over killing a duck.

After watching the ducks for a few minutes, she walked back to her car, leaving the ring on the edge of the gazebo for someone else to find. Maybe they'd have better luck with it than she had.

"How much for this frame, Ellie? I don't see a tag?" Lindsey waltzed up to Ellie's register, handing her a frame. "It was resting on the top of a trash can. Why would someone want to throw away such a beautiful frame?"

"Five bucks. It's a good cause, you know." Ellie's voice shook as she tried to sound casual. The janitors must have missed the trashcan under the tables last night when the sorting team finished.

"It would be great in Dylan's room, wouldn't it? With a new picture, perhaps?" Lindsey smiled.

"I'm sure it would look good in there. That's why I gave it to him, but you're welcome to more of my old stuff that I don't want anymore." Ellie smiled and handed the frame back to Lindsey.

"He just saved the best for last." Lindsey snatched the frame and stalked away. Ellie watched her go. Several comebacks flashed in her mind, but what did it matter now? Lindsey had "won," and the prize was exactly what Lindsey deserved.

When the sale was over, Ellie helped the rest of the team clean up, putting what was left into bags for a local shelter. The frame was back on the table. Ellie brought it over to Terrance York, who was counting the money. "Here's five for this frame."

She handed him the money and put the frame into her backpack. A frame that once had held her precious but now painful memories. Even though Dylan hadn't been her forever love, he had been her first love. She would write a scripture about healing on scrapbook paper and frame it, reminding her of what God had done through her heartbreak. A memorial of sorts, like those that guys in the Old Testament used to build every time God delivered them.

23

The beginning of Christmas break crept along, a nice change from the chaos of the fall semester. Casual friends no longer called, and her mom was worn out from chemo and the infection. Ellie spent most of her time filling out applications to Houston-area universities and finishing Christmas errands for her mom. Even though they were a little more thankful for each other this year, her family still seemed to be going through the motions of the holiday.

Their Christmas traditions were put on hold. Most of them included the Grants. Neither family had extended family around, so they had adopted each other. Since before she was born, the two families spent Christmas Eve together, and they alternated spending the night at each other's houses.

On the 23rd, Ellie's mom sat watching the lights on the tree, lost in her thoughts.

"Missing Mrs. Linda?"

"I'm fine, sweetie. Just fine." She brushed tears away with her fingers and put on a smile.

"Mom, we talked about being real, and that means admitting when you're sad." Ellie sat by her mom and patted her leg like Ellie was the parent.

"When did my baby girl get so smart?" She wrapped her arm around Ellie, holding her tight. "I miss Linda. She's more than just my friend. She's my sister. I always wanted one, and on our first double date with her and Robert, I knew I had found one."

"And it's all my fault." She leaned against her mom's chest, the way she had when her mom powers could still fix the world.

"No, don't say that. It's not even Dylan's fault even though your dad and I like to blame him. Linda and I put so much pressure on y'all to be a couple. You're still young, and Dylan has a lot of growing up to do." She pressed her lips to Ellie's hair.

"Love you, Mom, but I'm going to go get some fresh air."

"Sounds good. You've been cooped up too long. Check in later." She turned back to the tree.

On the way to her room, Ellie sent a text. Hopefully it would help make Christmas better for her mom. Grabbing her jacket and keys, she headed to Starbucks to wait. After a few minutes, he walked in. Her breath caught as old feelings threatened to surface. Even though he wore a black knit cap and a bulky jacket, making him like a thousand other guys in the city, she would recognize that walk anywhere. Long strides and a confident posture.

"What's up?" Dylan flipped a chair around, and sat, placing his arms on the chair's back.

"I got you your favorite." Ellie pushed the coffee toward him, not meeting his gaze.

"Some things never change, right?" He seemed as nervous and uncomfortable as she was. He reached out and touched her hand that was tapping on the table. "You still know me better than anyone else."

She jerked her hand away and tucked it safely under the table. "I doubt that. I didn't ask you to come for small talk or a walk down memory lane."

"What do you want then? I had plans for tonight but changed them for you."

"You know this has been a hard year for my family." Ellie took a sip of her latte.

"I'm not going to listen to a guilt trip. I get enough of those from my parents." He started to stand up.

"Just shut up, Dylan. Not everything is about you." He sat back down with his mouth hanging open, and she continued. "Not even talking about you, we've been through a lot with my mom's cancer, and I know she misses your mom."

"Yeah, my mom misses her too."

"So, we need to do something about it. Next year, we'll be off at college and moving on with our lives, but they will still be here, needing each other's friendships. The least we can do is put aside our hate for each other for one day to give them a happy Christmas."

His face softened at her words. "I've never hated you, Ellie. I was just so mad. I can't fix what I did to you, but you're right; they need each other. What're you thinking?"

For the next few minutes, they plotted. Dylan reached out to touch her hand again, but she leaned back in her chair, holding her cup. The move kept her a safe distance away but also meant she had nothing to look at but him. The way his eyes lit up as he laughed at some of their outlandish ideas for the scheme. His strong hands that had held hers so many times.

The history and the old feelings were almost palpable. *Get out before you do something stupid like take him back.* She got up mid-sentence and put her purse on her shoulder. "I guess I should go. I have a lot to do."

Surprise crossed Dylan's face, but he stood too. "Um, okay. I guess we can text tomorrow to double-check everything." He followed her to the door, holding it open for her. The place had been packed when she arrived, so her car was down at the end of the lot, near a stand of trees. "I'll walk you to your car."

Ellie picked up the pace, eager to get away from him, but his pace matched hers, his hand settled on her back. "You don't have to."

"I want to. A gentleman always walks a lady to her car."

"Well, here we are. Thanks for meeting me." Ellie unlocked the door and began pulling it open when Dylan pushed it shut with one hand. "What?"

She spun around to face him, which was a big mistake. He cupped her face with his hands and kissed her before she could react. His lips were soft and familiar. She instinctively brought her hands to his chest, counting his heartbeat beneath his toned muscles. He circled his arms around her waist and pulled her closer.

Pushing him away, she yelled, "What is wrong with you? What was that?" She touched her lips, still warm from his kiss.

"I don't know. Tonight was great. Like old times. I still love you." He reached out to touch her face.

"Are you kidding me? You're with Lindsey now. We're over."

"She's nothing. Nothing like you. You know you feel something too." His hand caressed her cheek.

Ellie swatted his hand away. "That's just memories, Dylan. When you've been with someone for so many years, it becomes comfortable and easy. If what we had was forever, you wouldn't have cheated."

"Why can't you forgive me for that? I've tried jumping through hoops, I've tried making you jealous with Lindsey. What more can I do?"

What? He had acted so cold when they broke up, like losing her was nothing, and here he was trying to get her back. He ran his fingers along her arm, reaching for her hand.

She let him hold her hand one last time. "Dylan, I don't feel the same way anymore. Yes, I felt something when we kissed, but I think it was only the memory of what we once felt. I'm moving on. It's been hard, lonely, and downright horrible, but it's what I need to do."

"Moving on with Josh, I see. What about me?" Dylan's eyes flashed.

"That's the thing. For once, I'm thinking about me, not you. We were just getting along ten minutes ago, planning what to do tomorrow. Can we just forget this happened?" Ellie opened her door.

"If that's what you want." Dylan stalked to his car but didn't get in. Instead, he stood watching her as she drove past, leaving him behind.

24

Ellie woke up early again. After her reaction to his kiss at the car, would Dylan back out of the plan? Returning from a morning run, she read a text from Dylan. He was doing his part, which was to convince his parents they should start a new tradition of going to a movie on Christmas Eve. After the movie, he was going to ask his parents to stop by the Lansing's house to drop off a donation for the mission trip that he had forgotten to turn in at school.

Ellie worked hard on her part, helping her mom cook as much food as they usually did despite only expecting the four of them. While the entree simmered and the desserts cooled, Ellie cleaned up so that her mom could relax. Just when it seemed like Dylan's family wouldn't get there before dinner, she got the text.

We're on our way.

She waited a few minutes to try to time the meet-up perfectly. "Mom, Dad, Nick, come down." The family's sluggishness had driven everyone to separate rooms, doing their own things.

"What do you want, Ellie? I'm in the middle of my game." Nick still had on his X-box headphone microphone.

As they all gathered, Ellie said, "You know, I was thinking, it's been a rough year on all of us, and this Christmas, we should be more thankful than usual. Mom's chemo's working, I finished my applications to a few schools here in town, Dad's job is great, and Nick. Well, I don't know what's good about Nick." She laughed when he play punched her. "Let's go outside, walk down the street and see the lights. I know this year is different, but it doesn't have to be bad. We can work up an appetite for dinner."

"You know, you're right." Her dad opened to the hall closet and passed out coats.

"I usually am. Let's go! I have mugs of hot chocolate we can drink as we walk." She pushed her family out the door. Dylan's parents were supposed to drive up as they walked out, but there was no sign of them, so she had to stall. It would be really annoying to be on the other end of the street and miss their chance. Thankfully, their neighbors went all out for Christmas decorations, so they had plenty to admire.

"This was a great idea, Ellie. My spirits are lifted already." Ellie's mom and dad held hands and smiled. "I'm thankful to be with my three favorite people."

"Is that Dylan's car? I wonder what he's doing here." Ellie tried to keep her voice natural.

"It is. That's odd." Her dad started walking to the car pulling into their driveway.

Dylan jumped out and headed toward the group. "Hi. I know y'all weren't expecting us, but I wanted to drop off something for the mission trip. It's nice to see y'all." He handed her the bag of school supplies he had to buy to make their plan work, and started back to the car, pausing to give Ellie time to do her part.

Ellie mom's gaze hadn't left the backseat where Linda sat. "Mom," she whispered. "Why don't we invite them in? Just for a few minutes."

Her mom shook her head. "No, I don't want you to be uncomfortable with Dylan around."

"It's okay." Ellie motioned for Mr. Grant to roll down the window. "Why don't y'all come in for a bit? We have plenty of food. I know you love my mom's pie."

After a few minutes of awkward back-and-forth, the two families settled into the living room. The ice was broken when Nick and Dylan's sister, Sydney, plugged in a Wii dance game and busted a few moves.

"We grabbed a bite before the movie, but this looks so good." Linda headed to the kitchen to help bring out the food. "I can't believe you cooked all this!"

"Ellie helped." The two women glanced at each other and then at Ellie before breaking out in grins.

"You knew they were coming, didn't you?" Ellie's mom pointed a finger at Ellie but smiled.

"We're caught." Dylan poked his head in the kitchen. "Mom, you were miserable without Mrs. L. We wanted y'all back together even if Ellie and I aren't."

His mom gave him a hug before moving on to Ellie. Mrs. Linda caught her in a warm, familiar embrace. Dylan apologized to Ellie's mom again. Her mom's reply was sweet and genuine. "All is forgiven."

During dinner, the adults picked up right where they had left off a few months ago. She and Dylan might not ever get to the point of being friends, and seeing him text on his phone, probably to Lindsey, still made her chest constrict, but her parents deserved to have their best friends back even if it meant she was uncomfortable the next few holidays. Dylan shot her a few glances over the table, but she broke contact. She couldn't go back now.

"You always put others' needs before your own. It's one of the best qualities about you." Her mom handed Ellie one of the fine China dinner plates to dry. The Grants had left a little while before, after a fun evening of Wii games and laughter, promising to see one another at the Martin family party the next night. "Thank you for tonight."

"It was hard. Seeing him, still caring about him, but knowing I have to move on. I stopped counting the times I wavered between wanting to run upstairs and cry or put my hand over his."

"That's normal. You loved him for a long time, and those feelings and habits don't go away quickly, but you made a big step tonight toward healing and forgiveness."

Taking a cup out of her mom's hand, Ellie dried a little more vigorously as she shared what happened when she and Dylan met to plan the surprise. "It's just harder than I thought, but Stacy's helping me."

She and Stacy had been meeting once a week at a cupcake shop for informal counseling and some coping mechanisms for when the pain sucked the very breath out of Ellie.

"I'm so glad. I don't want you to get to be my age and still wrestle with your issues from the past. Maybe I need to meet with Stacy too."

"She'd love to talk to you. I'll give you her number." The two worked in comfortable silence until the kitchen was clean.

Curled up on one of the couches, watching a movie with her family, Ellie pulled out her phone. There were a few mass 'Merry Christmas' texts from friends, but nothing from Josh even though she hadn't seen him in a few days. Although the break-up still stung, today had proven she would be fine with time, and she wanted to share that with Josh more than anyone else.

The next morning, Ellie woke up to shouts from Nick, who was eager to see if the guitar he had been hinting at wanting was under the tree. Grinning as Nick pulled her out of bed, she went with him to their parents' room to help him wake them up.

"Help, honey, the kids are attacking me." Their mom laughed as Nick and Ellie shook the mattress, as they had for years. Although they were too big to jump on the bed, Ellie was grateful they were able to share one more tradition for one more year. *I pray I'll never take these blessings for granted again.*

"I guess we can let them find the coal under the tree." Their dad got out of bed and put a wrestling hold on Nick as they stumbled down the stairs. Ellie and her mom took their time. Nick had already started passing out presents.

The next hour was a flurry of wrapping paper and strange sounds as Nick played his new guitar.

"Hopefully, one of those gifts left is some guitar lessons," Ellie teased.

"Or ear plugs for the rest of us." Ellie's mom covered her ears while Ellie's dad went to the kitchen to cook his famous waffles. After a leisurely breakfast and a few more hours of trying out their new gifts, Ellie went back upstairs to get ready to visit the Martins.

Christmas afternoon was a tradition. All the dads watched sports in the Martins' media room, the moms brought over all the leftovers, and the kids hung out, playing pool or the Wii in the game room or hanging out in the hot tub when it was a warm winter. The party was a farewell until school started again since most of the families took a vacation between Christmas and New Year's. The Martins had the best house for parties, and Cara said they had made it a cool place to hang out on purpose so that they could keep an eye on their kids. Dylan had told her he was going to Lindsey's house, so she was free to hang out in peace. Had he told her that to mess with her mind or to be kind?

Ellie took care getting dressed in dark jeans, leather boots, and a long pink sweater. She had bought Josh art supplies and tickets to two art galleries downtown. She took her own car over, going a little earlier than her parents to exchange gifts with Cara and Josh.

When she arrived, Josh's jeep wasn't there. Once inside the house, Ellie asked Cara about it.

Cara shrugged. "I don't know where he is; he just said he needed to clear his head. Who knows? I guess I've been a little distracted. I'm not so sure I can stick to my vow of not kissing until I wed. Those middle school books made it sound so easy!"

Listening to Cara gush about Mark, Ellie laughed. This is how her best friend must have felt all those years when Ellie recapped every detail of her date with Dylan. *I don't know how she lasted so long without slapping me back to reality.*

The two girls traded presents, and Ellie filled Cara in on the reconciliation effort. Friends started showing up, but Josh still wasn't home. Shoulders slumped, Ellie took his gift back to her car. She had wanted to give it to him in private. As she closed her trunk, his jeep pulled up and he seemed anything but excited to see her. She leaned back against her car and waited for him to get out.

"Merry Christmas, Josh." Ellie reached out to hug him, but he remained stiff and didn't return the embrace.

"You too." He stepped out of her arms and headed toward the door.

"What's the problem?"

"Nothing." He stopped but still didn't look at her.

"I was wondering why I hadn't heard from you the last few days, and now you're acting like I did something wrong." Ellie closed the gap between them, but he crossed his arms, keeping her out.

"Is Dylan here?"

"No. What does he have to do with anything? What'd he do now?"

Josh ran his fingers through his hair. "I thought you were moving past him, that you were moving forward maybe even with—" Josh stopped mid-sentence.

"I am moving past him." Ellie pulled him to the front yard swing where they had shared such a special moment not long ago. He walked with her but remained standing.

"Well, it didn't seem that way when I saw you at the coffee shop the other day. Or when I tried to stop by your house last night to give you your present, hoping you could explain what I saw, and there his car was in your driveway. What kind of hold does he have on you? Why do you keep going back to him? When are you going to realize you deserve better?"

Ellie stood up. "Are you kidding me? The only thing wrong with me is that I spent the last few months pouring out my heart to a guy who still thinks I'm weak, willing to take back a jerk because I'm not strong enough to be alone."

"I didn't mean that, but what do you expect me to think? I thought we were going somewhere. I told you I have feelings for you but would wait until you got over him. I thought you felt something, but then I see him kissing you." He sat down on the swing and put his head in his hands.

"Did you drive off before you saw me push him away? Look at me, Joshua." Ellie sat down next to him and put her arm on his shoulder, but he pulled away. He finally glanced at her, pain in his eyes. "I told him I don't feel that way anymore."

"It didn't seem like pulling away to me!" Josh leaned back on the swing and started rocking it.

"I was shocked at first." Ellie bit her lip. Josh had always been honest with her and deserved the same thing. "Look, we dated for years. I loved him. So, yes, I didn't pull away at first. It was comfortable and familiar."

She sat sideways in the swing, but he kept his head leaned back on the top of the swing, just listening. "But as soon as I realized what was happening, I stopped it."

"I don't want to be your rebound boyfriend. We've been spending time together, and maybe you're just lonely."

"You're not. Right now, you're my best friend." If only she had the words to tell him how important he was, how much his friendship meant to her.

"See, when we hang out, you're thinking about friendship, and I'm thinking about how beautiful you are and how much I care about you." Josh stood up. "I don't want to pressure you, but I am not going to be a fill-in while you and Dylan figure things out."

"I already know I don't want him." Ellie stood up too, and he backed away.

"But, you kissed him back, and you need to figure all that out before we can have a shot at anything. I'm not walking away because I don't like you, I'm walking away because I do like you. I told you I'd wait, but I don't want to be played or start something you can't finish." He tucked his hands into his jacket pockets, giving her one last look before he got into his jeep and drove off.

Watching him go, Ellie's heart sank. Josh was everything she had always pretended Dylan was. She sat there, watching for his jeep to turn around. For him to come back. But he didn't.

25

The longer she sat in her bedroom chair waiting for Josh to text her, the faster her foot tapped the hardwood floor. She had never led him on, never flirted. Well, except that one time after the football game. They had shared some sweet moments where something could have happened, but she had never crossed the friendship line. It wasn't her fault that he felt more. Yeah, she had kind of thrown herself at him the night she got drunk. Okay, maybe she had led him on or hinted there was something more. She had ridden an emotion roller coaster the last few months, and she had taken him along for the ride. But, that didn't give him the right to be mad. He knew what she was going through and shouldn't expect her to have everything figured out.

She'd left his present in front of his bedroom door, but he hadn't even texted her about that. She replayed their conversation in her mind. When he had described seeing her and Dylan kissing, his face had twisted in pain. *And I expected him to comfort me like his feelings weren't involved.*

Finally, she sent him a text. I'm really sorry.

Ellie waited for a response, but one didn't come. She put her phone down and wrote in her journal, getting her emotions out instead of pretending they didn't exist, like Stacy had suggested, before ending with her devotional for the day. When she got into bed with a book, she found a text at last.

`After Cara texted Mark for the 100`th` time, Dad threatened to throw our phones out the window if we were texting. See you on the mission trip.`

Maybe some time apart would be good.

A second text came through a minute later. `Thanks  for the awesome present.`

So that was that. Ellie turned back to her romance novel. It wasn't an invitation to visit the art museum with him, but it was better than silence.

Because most of the class was out of town, it was up to Ellie and a few other students to gather the remaining donations and organize them at the school with their senior class sponsors. Three years' worth of planning came together to make the week fly by. She spent each morning visiting area churches, picking up the donations. The afternoons were spent shopping for the remaining supplies with the class treasurer, Celeste Divall.

The planning committee had mapped out each day's activities, but she and Celeste had a blast picking out crafts and games to go with each lesson. When they browsed the paint section, Ellie couldn't help but think of Josh and their paint date. She hadn't heard from him again, but that was for the best. *I don't even know how I feel, much less what to say.*

Dylan had called to hang out once, claiming to want to see her as friends, but she had told him no. Lindsey was out of town, and Ellie wouldn't be Lindsey's substitute.

After Ellie and Celeste bought all the materials, they spent the rest of the week organizing. While they worked, Celeste said, "You know, you're really good at this."

"At what?" Ellie put down her clipboard and faced her friend.

"Organizing stuff. I've had fun, but I like the numbers game, figuring out how much we can buy, what to spend the money on. You, on the other hand, see the big picture. How the stuff will be used, organizing it, managing the people and their duties." Celeste pointed to the boxes that were labeled by day and type of material.

"It's been more fun than I pictured when I signed up, that's for sure." Ellie beamed.

"Well, you'd be a great event planner." Celeste turned back to the box she was packing. Cara had said that too. Perhaps her friends were on to something. The two worked in silence until they'd crossed off everything on the to-do list.

While their parents celebrated New Year's Eve with a small group of friends, Ellie talked Nick into joining her at a youth group gathering at Stacy's church, which Ellie now called her own. The youth group had embraced her for her, not who her boyfriend was or her social status at school. In fact, she had never mentioned Dylan other than to share during prayer requests that she was dealing with a difficult break-up.

Nick had been going through a rough time, and their mom's cancer hadn't been easy on him. Hopefully he would get involved in the group too, even if it meant her sometimes annoying brother would be hanging out with her. As soon as they arrived, he recognized a few guys from his football league who greeted him with fist bumps. Ellie smiled and walked over to her new friends.

As midnight approached, Stacy and Micah called everyone to the chairs arranged in a huge circle. After praying, they passed out sheets of paper and pens.

A few of the guys muttered under their breath about having to write at a party. Opening his Bible, Micah began to read from II Corinthians chapter 5. He paused and repeated verse 17 two more times. "Therefore, if anyone is in Christ, he is a new creation; the old has gone, the new has come!" When he finished the next verse, he paused.

"Often, we focus on New Year's resolutions and what we're going to do differently. We make lists of how we can be better, but scripture tells us we are already new. The old is gone in an instant." Micah spoke with passion and conviction.

"We know it's hard to shake the past. Sometimes we hang on to our own sin. Sometimes it's other people's sin that we can't forgive. For the next few minutes, I want you to reflect on the past year or years. Write down what you're still angry about, what has hurt you, the disappointments, the sin, the failure. Write it all down." Micah put on some soft praise music.

"I may need more paper," said Michael, the group's clown.

A few items came quickly. Her mom's cancer. Dylan. Amelia. Lindsey. She stared at her list, full of other people's names. She had spent the last few months blaming everyone except herself for the pain in her life. Her pride that insisted on looking perfect to others. The idol she'd created out of Dylan and their relationship. She hadn't tried to figure out what made Lindsey such a mean person. Without concern for Josh's feelings, she'd expected him to fill the hole Dylan left in her heart.

Ellie tried to blink back the tears as she filled up the page. Wiping her tears, she glanced around. Many were still writing while others sat with their heads bowed. Some had tearstains on their cheeks too. *I'm not alone.*

When most of the group had finished, Micah and Stacy asked the group to follow them outside. The cold night's strong wind pricked Ellie's face as she walked toward the huge cast-iron chimenea on the edge of the parking lot. After the group gathered around the fire, Micah prayed, thanking God that they were new creatures at the moment of salvation and asking for God to do amazing things in them and through them in the coming year as they let go of their sins and hurts from the past year.

Stacy spoke up. "This year was hard on us. You all know we had a miscarriage this summer, and I've had so much anger and sorrow over our loss. I am choosing to let that go, so I can be open and ready for what God has next, whether that's a biological baby, an adopted one, or even no baby at all." Micah held her close, kissing her on the forehead as she dropped her paper in the fire.

"Just like my beautiful bride let go of the past, I want you to drop your lists in the fire. Let go of the past failures so that you can be whole for God to use this new year." He dropped in his own paper and stepped back.

Ellie's hands shook as she brought her list to the flames. She had been dragging around Dylan's sin and the disease that ravaged her mom's body like a child who couldn't let go of her security-blanket, blaming anything that didn't go right on them. But, more than anything, a new start meant saying goodbye to the past that had haunted her for months. She watched the flames turn the crisp white paper into ashes that sank to the bottom, mixing until she could no longer differentiate what had been her burden from the others.

Sitting down in one of the chairs around the fire, they began their countdown to the next year and the beginning of the fireworks show the guys had been talking about all night. Nick sat down next to her halfway through the displays of color and noise and handed her a cup of hot chocolate.

"Are you sure you want to be seen with your sister?"

"You're not so bad, especially since you broke up with Dylan." Nick watched the fireworks instead of her.

"Why do you say that?" Ellie took a sip. Nick had been so rude to Dylan the first day of school and had plenty of snide comments when they broke up.

"You were boring with him. Everything was about him. You were turning into Mom, wanting to be perfect more than being happy." Wow, her brother, who told her he loved her once a year on her birthday, was opening up. He ducked his head.

"Well, all that's in the fire now." Ellie nudged his arm.

"Good. Too bad we couldn't throw Dylan in there."

"Maybe you should have put that on your list."

"I did, but you can't expect miracles overnight, can you?" He stood up and gave her a wink that she had caught him practicing in the mirror.

Ellie finished her hot chocolate and settled back in her chair, watching the beautiful colors light up the sky. What was God going to do in her life, starting with the mission trip in two days?

26

Ellie jumped out of bed before her alarm went off and took a quick shower. She dressed in yoga pants and a t-shirt for a full day of traveling. She barely made it through the breakfast her parents made before they prayed over her, asking for protection and for God to do a great work.

Double-checking her bags one more time, Ellie and her parents packed up the car for the drive to school. Several students and parents were already there, including Cara and Josh who were talking with friends. How would he act around her? Would he be distant while waiting to see if she would crawl back to Dylan, or friendly like the last few months? Or, would he give her one of those looks that showed he had feelings but would wait for her to be ready? Which one would be the worst? Although distant or casual would hurt, could she handle seeing how he felt, knowing he wasn't going to act on his feelings?

Josh was dressed as usual: jeans, a Waltham football sweatshirt, and Texans' hat. But there was something different. His crooked smile lit up when he saw her car. His brown eyes shone as they connected with hers. Her heart jumped. But he turned back to the crowd.

Cara waved and waited for Ellie to open her door. "Hey, Lansing family."

The two girls hugged as if they hadn't seen each other in months. "Josh, come help. Ellie has some of the supplies for the trip."

Cara struggled to pull out Ellie's heavy suitcases. Josh's laid-back stride quickened as he walked over to help. His eyes never left hers, but he didn't say much, other than hi to her parents.

Ellie fiddled with the zipper on her jacket. They stared at each other awkwardly for a second. Josh grabbed one of supply bags and walked with her dad to the buses where the class sponsors were loading the luggage.

Joined by her mom, Ellie carried the backpack she would keep with her and followed them. "That was a little awkward. Should I be worried about you, Ellie?"

"He's been such a good friend to me with the whole Dylan situation, but he thinks I need to get over Dylan before something can happen with us." Ellie watched Josh and her dad talking. "He kinda reminds me of Dad. Strong. Loyal. Loves Jesus."

Ellie had told her mom about her growing feelings for Josh but not about how things ended Christmas day. Her mom would probably try to make all of Ellie's emotions fit into a beautifully wrapped box instead of accepting them for the confusing mess they were.

"I can see that. I pushed you into a relationship with Dylan, wanting the fairy tale romance Linda and I had dreamed of since we were pregnant. I'm not going to make that mistake again. You follow Jesus, Ellie, and I know He will bring the right guy along. Maybe soon. Maybe later. But, it will be His time." Her mom gave her a hug as they neared the group.

Ellie whispered in her mom's ear, "I won't rush things, I promise. Some things are worth waiting for."

The rest of the students were gathering, and the group joined hands to pray. Ellie hugged her parents one more time and promised to text and send pictures often. After her parents drove away, Ellie headed inside to the bathroom before getting onto the bus for the next twelve hours.

She must have walked in quietly because the girls in the stalls didn't quit talking.

"I can't wait for ten uninterrupted days with Dylan." Ellie groaned inwardly. Lindsey. "I've missed him so much this week while we were on vacation. With no parents around, we can spend as much time together as we want."

"I don't think that's the point of the trip." Melissa responded.

Why did girls think they could talk freely in the bathroom, clueless anyone could hear?

"Well, that's the point for me. He's so wonderful. He told me this morning—" The sound of flushing water and the stall doors opening drowned out the words.

"Are you sure that's just not because he wanted more than what you were giving? You know guys will tell you anything to get what they want."

Ellie grinned at Melissa's bluntness. If she wasn't such good friends with Lindsey, she might be a nice person. A group of girls walked in, laughing and talking, and Lindsay's conversation was over.

Ellie waited a few minutes before coming out so that Lindsay wouldn't see her. And she needed a few moments to catch her breath. Although she didn't want Dylan anymore, it still stung that he was already making promises to Lindsey. *Especially since he kissed me a week ago and said Lindsey meant nothing.* One more reason it was best she was moving on, even if it hurt.

Dylan and Lindsay's relationship would not ruin Ellie's trip. She held her head high as she strode past them to line up for the bus that would carry them toward Arizona and then across the border to Sonora, Mexico. She relaxed her shoulders when Dylan and Lindsey lined up to get into another bus. They were holding hands. When Lindsey glared at her, Ellie forced a smile. Lindsey held her gaze and leaned her head on Dylan's shoulder. When he brought his other arm around her in a hug, Lindsey finally smiled back.

"Don't let them get to you. You know one of the main reasons she's with him is because of you." Cara waved to Lindsey. "That's why I try to kill her with kindness."

Ellie grinned. "Whoever said that, did they mention how long it takes for that to work?"

"Not quick enough for this trip." It was their turn to board the bus.

Mark pointed at the bench in front of him, "We saved y'all a seat." Cara sat down in front of Mark, who sat next to Josh. Cara motioned for Ellie to sit by her.

The girls thanked Mark, and Ellie gave Josh a grin as she got settled. *How am I going to last all day next to him without asking him how he feels?*

Cara faced the guys. "This is going to be amazing."

The rest of the day was spent in a cycle of listening to music, chatting with Cara, playing silly car games, watching Josh draw, and taking naps. When Mark and Cara moved down the bus to talk to some other friends, Ellie turned to talk to Josh. He smiled but put on his headphones and plugged them into his iPhone. Switchfoot's "Love Alone is Worth the Fight" blared through the speakers and Ellie smiled, leaving their conversation for another day. That was his choice if he wanted to burst his eardrums just to ignore her.

"I took four naps today, but all I want to do is sleep." Ellie ducked into the bathroom to change into her pajamas. She and Cara were lucky to be sharing a room. Amanda was with them as well as Melissa, who seemed uncomfortable with the arrangement.

"Me too." Melissa yawned. "Our bus was so boring, but I couldn't sleep. It seemed like the couples bus, and I was the odd girl out." It was obvious who the main couple was. Melissa started digging in her bag, avoiding eye contact.

"Hey," Amanda interjected. "Xavier and I were talking to everyone. Plus, there's always Ethan. He was flirting with you."

"Are you kidding me? He flirts with his reflection in the rearview mirror. I'm lonely, not desperate." Melissa leaned back on the bed, turning on her side to face the girls.

Cara gave Melissa a hug. "I know how you feel. I was the third wheel for years. It can be hard even when you're happy being single."

Melissa's phone rang, and she stepped off to the side, but the little room meant every word was clear. "I'm not covering for you. Mrs. Gunning told us they would be doing room checks."

Amanda and Ellie gave each other a look, but Cara was the one who whispered, "Lindsey."

"Everyone knows he's going out with her to make you jealous. It's pathetic." Amanda sat down on the bed and pulled out her phone. "I bet Xavier has already texted me about it. Dylan's his boy, but we're both getting tired of this."

Lindsey must have been talking a while, but Melissa finally broke in. "Enough. I'm not doing it."

"Let's talk about something else. If Lindsey's stupid enough to sneak out and do whatever, she deserves what she gets." Ellie's words came out harsher than she meant. If anyone knew how loving Dylan could make you feel, it was her.

"Yes, let's." Melissa switched her phone off and tossed it on the bed. "I'm not getting in trouble for her. I've looked forward to this trip for too long to risk getting sent home." The rest of the evening was spent talking about the trip, college, and any other topic besides guys.

The next day was another day of driving, but this time, the chaperones ordered the guys onto one bus and the girls onto the other. They pulled out of the hotel parking lot at six a.m., and Ellie was groggy. She put on her headphones and leaned against her pillow on the window, but sleep eluded her.

As they were getting ready this morning, Melissa had turned on her phone to what must have been a long list of messages from Lindsey. As she read, Melissa's head shook and then she began to mutter under her breath. "Stupid. Stupid girl. I told her

I wouldn't cover for her, thinking she would be smart enough to stay put in her room."

No one asked her about it, but it was obvious Lindsey had snuck out to meet Dylan. Then, as they were getting in the van, Dylan kept his arms tightly wrapped around Lindsey until a teacher came and told them to let go.

They must not have gotten caught, but Mrs. Gunning's voice was stern and annoyed when she announced they would split up for the rest of the drive. What had happened between the two of them the night before? The casual way he had moved on cheapened their history, like their relationship meant nothing to him when its end had rocked her to the core.

Ellie finally drifted off, and when she woke a few hours later, the view out of the window featured mountains. They were getting close. Josh was probably busy sketching the beautiful landscape. She started a text, asking him what he was drawing, but exited her messages and switched over to Instagram. She smiled. He had just posted a picture of the sunrise. His caption read `Good painting material`. She clicked 'Like'.

After typing and deleting three times, she posted a comment on his picture. `It's amazing`. She kept refreshing to see if he would reply to her comment, but he didn't. Who were they kidding that they could just act as if the last few months hadn't happened? Refreshing the picture one more time, she was done pretending.

Ellie twisted one of her curls as they approached the border. All the students held their passports and grew quiet. Some kids who had gone to Mexico on mission trips before warned that border agents might require payment for entrance into the country, but the agent who checked their bus simply poked his head in at the driver's side window, smiled as everyone held up their passports, and waved them in.

After a day and a half of traveling, Ellie's legs screamed for a good stretch and a run. Soon they left paved roads and drove down bumpy dirt. The sun was just starting to set as they entered a small town. Golden rays reflected off the mountains. The skyline was magnificent.

In contrast to the rich sky, the poverty of the shack-lined streets pulled at her heart. Some were pieces of metal leaning against each other. Kids playing outside stopped to watch the buses drive past. Their faces were covered in dirt and many were not dressed for the cold weather, but their smiles were bright and their hands eager as they waved. Could they see her through the tinted windows? She grinned back and waved.

27

Minutes later, they reached the gate at the entrance of the orphanage on the outskirts of the small town. A playground was surrounded by four buildings. One for the fifty orphans, one for activities, and two smaller dorms for visiting missions groups. The buildings were plain brick but clean. The class sponsors passed out candy for the teens to give to the kids, easing the introductions. Ellie clutched her bag and stepped out of the bus.

As they walked through the fence, the air was filled with the squeals of young children and their footsteps as they ran to greet the teens. Most of the kids ran up and gave hugs to the teens, but some stood aside and watched. Thankful for years of Spanish classes, Ellie approached one girl who hung back, offering a hello and a piece of candy. The girl took the candy but didn't look Ellie in the eye as she sat down in the dirt next to a tree. Ellie tried to talk to the girl, but she didn't offer more than her name. Naomi.

As Naomi ate her piece of candy, Ellie studied her. About five or six, Naomi had curly black hair that was a frizzy mess, just like Ellie's usually was. Her wide brown eyes stared at the ground, but when she smiled, she was missing her two front teeth. Ellie kept up a one-sided conversation. When she finished her sucker, Naomi climbed into Ellie's lap and started talking a mile a minute, pointing to the kids and laughing at the guys, who had pulled out the soccer balls and started a game with the older children. It was tough keeping up with Naomi's rapid Spanish.

When the dinner bell rang, Naomi pulled Ellie's hand, asking her to eat at her table. The orphans had decorated for their visitors. There were brightly colored streamers and children's drawings hanging on the walls of a long dining room that held twelve tables and ten highchairs. The dinner was buffet style, with the kids lining up on both sides of a long table to scoop up beans, rice, and a pork dish. Grabbing a cup of punch, Ellie followed Naomi to a table. When everyone was seated, the head of the orphanage, a large woman named Ruby, prayed. "Lord, thank you for everything. Thank you for this group. Bless them. Bless the food."

Her simple prayer in broken English was honest and sincere. When was the last time Ellie had just asked God for something instead of talking to Him like a lawyer, presenting a list of all the good things she had done to earn what she wanted?

While they ate, Ellie asked the kids questions and showed them pictures of her family on her iPhone. In spite of their hardships, the orphans laughed, joked, and told stories of the day, happy to have a captive audience. The boy across the table begged Ellie to let him play a game on her phone. *I guess we're not so different after all.*

Dinner ended too quickly, and Ruby told the kids it was time for their nightly routines. The younger kids had to get ready for bed as the older ones did homework. Ellie carried dishes to the sink where two workers were busy washing the growing pile. Naomi was still attached to her, holding on to

Ellie's shirt. Ellie knelt down and promised Naomi she would see her when she got home from school the next day. Naomi wrapped her arms around Ellie's neck in a strong embrace. *I could have used a hug like this a few weeks ago.* Ellie held her new friend for a minute more before returning to the bus to unpack.

It took an hour just to unload the buses and then two more hours to organize the crates of supplies into the dorms and activity room. During the day, while the older orphans were at school, the teens would be busy with repairs, household chores, and the babies. When the kids came home from school, the real fun would begin.

After the activity stations were set up, Ellie retreated to her dorm room with Cara, Amanda, and Melissa. Celeste and Emma joined them in a room with three sets of bunk beds with hard mattresses. They unpacked the linens they had brought and made their beds as they shared their experiences of the day. All six of them had the same first impression—amazement at the happiness and love that oozed out of kids whose lives were so drastically different from the comfortable lives the teens had. Before going to bed, the girls prayed together. *Is this how dorm life at a Christian college might be?*

As they got into their beds to spend some time writing in their journals, Ellie sent a text to her parents and Nick, sharing a picture she had snapped of her and Naomi. She received three responses within two minutes, but her mom's cracked her up.

Put her in your suitcase and bring her home to me. I'll need another girl when you go off to college.

The next morning, the girls woke up to banging on the door, shouting in Spanish, and laughing. They raced to the dining room. The kids were dressed in their school uniforms, wanting to say goodbye before heading off for the day. After passing out hugs, the girls dressed and headed to the workers' kitchen for breakfast and devotionals. Not wanting to be a burden to the orphanage, the group brought their own breakfast and lunch supplies. They'd eat dinner with the kids each evening to build relationships.

Wanting to have flexibility to check on other groups and make sure the supplies were ready for each day, Ellie had signed up for housework help. One of the housekeepers, Leticia, led her to the laundry room. Piles and piles of clothes and towels were dumped on a dirty floor. Ellie stared at the three washers and dryers and then back at the piles of clothes. Cara might find her body buried under an avalanche of laundry.

Ellie grabbed the towels to wash first. That would give her time to sort the rest of the piles. Laundry here was a bit more complex than at home. After loading the washers and adding detergent the team brought, she used the hose from outside to fill up the washer faster. Afterwards, she organized the clothes into eighteen loads of laundry. Fifty kids, plus four full-time, live-in workers produced a lot of dirty clothes.

After sorting, she looked around. There were shelves lining the walls. Each shelf was labeled with a child's name and filled with piles of clothes. Their rooms must be tiny not to even have space for their clothes. Her walk-in closet at home was full of clothes she didn't even wear. *Can't change that now. Focus on here and now.* The washer finished, and Ellie switched loads. The piles on the floor didn't appear any smaller. It was going to be a long morning.

Ellie didn't leave the laundry room for the rest of the day, using the time the washers and dryers were running to clean the room. She started with folding and organizing each shelf that had clothes thrown on it. Then she wiped down the windows that were covered with the dust that coated everything here in the desert. She laughed at herself. She was creating more stuff to wash by using towels. Finally, when the piles that lined the floor diminished, she worked on the floor, sweeping and mopping. Her arms ached and her clothes were dirty, but the room sparkled.

When the kids returned from school with gleeful shouts, Ellie left the laundry room and headed outside, meeting up with Cara and the rest of the craft crew. Her eyes searched for Josh, but he wasn't in the group working on the construction or the crowd hanging around talking to the kids. Was he avoiding her?

"I don't know if I'll ever have kids." Cara's shirt featured several splotches. Some were colored and some just looked wet. She pointed to each one and explained. "Spit up. Throw up. Banana. Something orange they ate. I'm tired."

"Me too. I spent the day with laundry. Exciting times. My arms feel like they are about to fall off, and we haven't even started the fun."

Amanda ambled up. "Let's get set-up while they eat their after-school snack." The three girls laid out the craft tables to decorate picture frames. The lesson was on how special the kids were in God's eyes, and the kids would get to pose for pictures, which they would put in the frames they decorated at the art station. The teens had been told that most of the kids didn't have pictures of themselves, so Mrs. Collins, the yearbook and journalism teacher, brought her camera and photo printer.

When the kids came into the room, Naomi ran straight for Ellie, who knelt down to receive her hug. After a lesson, it was singing time. Enough seniors had musical talent that they were able to create a band, using the donated instruments kept in a closet for mission groups. Jonathan Sanders, the senior class president and a guy they all joked would be a pastor one day, led worship. He switched back and forth from English to Spanish. Ellie closed her eyes as he sang in Spanish about how great God is. The voices of the orphans surrounded her. Surely this is what heaven would be like. Different cultures, different languages, one God.

The songs ended and Ellie was bombarded with kids wanting to decorate frames. Some of the frames just needed stickers, which is what she was helping with, while others needed painting. Josh was helping the kids paint. She watched while he helped a boy paint a soccer ball on his frame. They were both laughing. Josh's face shone and already had paint smudges. He met her gaze. Caught staring, she blushed. He gave her a smile and turned back to the boy.

The rest of the afternoon flew by in a whirl of stickers, sequins, and glue as the kids made their frames before going outside for the pictures. The sky was once again a beautiful orange as the sun sank behind the mountains, providing the perfect picture backdrop. The loud music that came from nearby houses created a fun atmosphere for posing and playing. After cleaning up her station, Ellie sat off to the side, watching a few kids beg to be in more pictures.

Some of the older kids were shy, blushing and ducking their heads, but the younger kids hammed it up. Some wanted to be photographed on the orphanage's playground equipment, hanging from monkey bars or swinging. Most American moms would cringe at the jagged edges of the metal equipment, disasters waiting to happen, but the kids played without a care or an accident.

After another fun supper in the midst of loud conversation, Ellie returned to the laundry room, now re-covered in clothes and towels from the younger kids' showers. Fighting sleepiness, she started another load. Afterwards, she sat on the dryer and gazed out of the window. The older kids who had finished their homework were outside, playing until the last light faded. They had started a game of soccer, and Josh was running in the middle of the field, arms stretched upward as his teammate scored a goal.

"Hiding out?" Cara's words broke Ellie's thoughts.

Ellie pointed to the piles of clothes that lined the floor. "Trying to get a head start on tomorrow's work. They just dropped off the little kids' clothes from today."

"Yeah, it seemed we spent a good amount of time changing their clothes as they ruined them—and ours. We didn't get to talk much today. How was your day?" Cara climbed on top of the other dryer and looked out too.

"Full of laundry. Who knew washing clothes could be an all-day gig." Ellie leaned her head against the wall and kept watching the guys. It was now dark, and the group had moved to the lighted area, hanging out on the merry-go-round and swings.

"I know. Taking care of babies all day isn't glamorous, but I could feel God's presence. Like it pleased Him."

"I felt the same thing. It was just me in here, washing and folding clothes, but I felt like I was doing His work. You know, some of the older girls have to help do the laundry every evening. My doing it gives them a week off to enjoy being kids." Ellie turned to Cara, forcing herself not to stare at Josh anymore.

"So, I know I've always stayed out of the middle of things, but what's up with you and my brother?" Cara pulled a small bag of chocolates out of her pocket and offered some to Ellie.

"You're hoping to bribe me into telling all?" Ellie took a piece despite her protests.

"Well, y'all were getting close before Christmas, but I didn't want to bring it up. Now, y'all just look at each other but don't talk."

"Yeah, I noticed you were staying clear of us when we hung out. Or, you were just too involved with Mark," Ellie teased.

"Don't change the subject. It's cool if you don't want to say anything, but y'all seem to be avoiding each other. I'm here if you want to talk."

The two girls were silent for a bit. Cara was comfortable with silence and patient in listening. Finally, Ellie poured out what had been going on. She looked out the window during her monologue but turned to see her friend smiling and doing a little shoulder dance.

"I knew y'all had feelings for each other."

"I think I like him." Ellie told her what happened on New Year's Eve. "But, he's right. Even though Dylan is already 'in love' with Lindsey, I don't think you can just jump into a relationship after years with someone else. That wouldn't be fair to Josh when I'm so confused. Maybe I should take time for myself. With my mom's cancer, Dylan, graduation, college, and now my feelings for Josh. It's too much."

"First, Dylan is not in love with Lindsey, no matter what story she spins in her little deluded mind." Cara stood up as the washer finished. She started moving items to the dryer and continued, "Second, I think y'all are doing the right thing taking things slowly. If he's avoiding you, it's because he thinks that's what he's supposed to do to give you time to move on from Dylan. And, it's okay if that takes a long time."

"Yeah, but it's so hard because I know I don't want to be with Dylan. I see Josh, and I want to talk to him, to be around him, and I don't want to hurt him when I know how much he cares for me. But, I miss him. He's been a good friend." Ellie closed her dryer door and turned it on before loading the washer again.

"That's why I avoided relationships, but I think I learned something being single for so long." Cara leaned against the washer, watching Mark, who was swinging as high as he could and then flipping off the seat, no doubt teaching the kids bad habits. "I'm comfortable alone or with Mark. I know who I am without him."

"But you're happier with him," Ellie teased. Cara, who had always said women shouldn't get married until they had their college degree and a few years of working under their belts, would probably beat her to the altar.

"Yep. But, seriously, take as much time as you need to figure out who you are by yourself. Get comfortable in your own skin. If you're meant to be with Josh, it will happen in God's time." Cara pulled Ellie toward the door. "That's enough work for today. Let's go out and have some fun. We need to show Mark how to do a real flip off a swing. Cheerleader style."

28

The next two days were filled with laundry, lessons, singing, and crafts. Leticia had complimented Ellie on how she organized the laundry room. Ellie moved on to setting up the storage room next door while the loads ran. Laundry and a cleaned-out room weren't much, but it was a weight off Leticia. Ellie rehearsed the scripture where Jesus told the disciples that the good they did to the least of these was done unto Him. As she cleaned the laundry room floor for the sixth time in three days, she prayed her work would honor God. Leticia's hug answered her prayer.

The group fell into a routine, and Naomi became Ellie's shadow. Every day after school, Naomi found Ellie in the laundry room and dragged her outside. During their playtime, Naomi told the story of how her parents had died in a car crash along with her little brother. Naomi couldn't remember much about them and only had one picture of her family. She had been only three.

Holding Naomi on her lap in a swing, Ellie's chest ached. Her mom was battling a life-threatening disease, but poor Naomi had never had a chance to get to know hers. Naomi's squeals as they soared through the air broke the somber moment. Ellie kicked her legs to make them go higher and faster. *Dear God, one day I would like to adopt a little girl like Naomi or help other orphans find a permanent home.*

That night, the guys built a bonfire, showing the kids how to roast hotdogs and marshmallows. Some of the girls were making s'mores. Chocolate streaks covered most of the kids' faces as they glowed in the light of the fire.

Ellie's spirit stirred. God promised he had a purpose, a plan just for her. Maybe it was with orphans. Kids like the ones here. Angels who smiled despite having very little, who shared what little they had with the others, who were content with yearly visits from churches from the United States. The when, where, or how of her purpose wasn't crystalized yet, but that was okay. Her new dream for her life featured just herself and God, which was now more important than anything else.

Ellie snapped a few pictures of the children, sending them to her parents with a quick text telling them she felt called to help orphans. Pressing send, she looked up, connecting with Josh. They had done a good job of avoiding each other, but this time, he didn't break eye contact. His brown eyes pierced hers in the fading glow of the sunset. Even though he walked away, giving her space, his eyes said he still cared. Instead of breaking his gaze, she smiled bigger and gave him a little wave. He lifted a hand and then turned when the boy sitting next to him asked him a question.

Many of the kids had gone inside to get ready for bed, but most of the senior class stayed around the fire, singing worship songs as a few guys strummed guitars. Only two more full days. It would be hard to go back home, and she would be leaving a part of her heart behind. The fire ebbed, and only a few people remained. Just when she was about to get up and go inside, Josh sat next to her. She remained silent.

He shifted, starting to talk but stopping several times. "I miss you, Lansing."

"Me too." Ellie brought her knees up to her chest and rested her chin on her knees. Josh got up. Was he leaving already? Instead, he threw another log into the fire, bringing it back to life.

"Figured we may be here a little while." He sat down, this time a little to the side so that he was facing her. They sat in silence, watching the flames. Because of their last conversation, she would have to be the one to say something about their relationship or lack thereof. Josh wasn't going to push. The ball was in her court, and she was letting it bounce until it simply rolled away.

When the last embers died out, Josh jumped to his feet, reaching out for her hand and pulling her up. His hands were warm and rough from a week of rebuilding a room, painting, and cleaning up the brush around the orphanage. He held her hand as they headed back to the girls' dorm, but halfway to the door he let go.

"I enjoyed your company."

Ellie turned to face him. His cheeks were flushed from the fire, and his hair was disheveled from the cold wind. "Well, we didn't talk much."

"You don't always need words to talk, Ellie. I'm willing to wait until you know what you want to say." He gave her a quick hug, and Ellie walked into her room, full of things to write in her journal, feelings she wasn't quite ready to share with anyone.

On the final full day, Ellie woke before the sun was even up. All week, she had wanted to wake up to see if the sunrise was as beautiful as the sunset, and each morning, she failed. Today she wanted to enjoy every moment. She took a shower, dressed in jeans and a warm sweater, and grabbed a banana and her journal before slipping outside without waking anyone up.

It was still dark when she walked to one of the benches set up near the area marked as a baseball / soccer field. The sky lit up the surrounding mountains with morning glory. Purple preceded the brilliance of the sun's greeting. "Beautiful job, Jesus."

She took a few pictures, trying to capture the beauty but they would never do it justice. Instead, she wrote in her journal.

I can't believe You created this universe and yet knew I would be here in this moment, marveling at what you spoke into existence. I once thought You boring, a God who gave lists of rules and rewarded people for following them. This trip has proven You are so much more. There's pain here, but the beauty is even more powerful. I can't even put it into words, so I'm leaving room to put a picture later. I just want to remember this moment — feeling Your love cover me in the first glimmers of morning.

Your love. I've been so wrapped up in my idea of loving Dylan, but I had no idea what love is. Thank you for showing me how much I have in my life. Thank you for giving me a glimpse of your plan for my life. I know it will be so much better than the plans I had to follow a guy around. These kids have shown me that I don't have to have a popular boyfriend and a perfect family to be happy. You've shown me a purpose in life, a way to serve you instead of myself. And I'm excited to get to know myself better as I get to know you in a more personal, realistic way. Thank you so much for opening my eyes.

Just then, the sun rose fully over the mountains, spreading its rays over the orphanage. Josh was sitting on the monkey bars, his Bible open. His face was at peace, as he always was when he was doodling in one of his notebooks. He was ready to work, wearing paint-stained jeans and an old sweatshirt. He bowed his head, moving his lips in prayer.

Wow, I want him to hold me, comfort me like he has so many times. But even more, I want to be whole.

When he seemed through with his prayer, Ellie moved to him to tell him what was on her heart. "So, I've decided what I want to do with my life." She giggled when he flinched and almost lost his balance.

He recovered, grabbing the bar in front of him right before he slipped off. "And what's that?"

"I want to work somewhere, somehow to help kids in situations like this. Or even these kids. I have no clue what kind of degree or job it is, but that's what I want to do. People need to know about these kids, and I want to share their stories." Ellie climbed up the monkey bars until she was sitting across from him. Not close enough to touch but near enough that her heart beat faster.

"And you would be awesome at that." Josh grinned.

"For so long, I thought of my future in relation to Dylan's future. I never even pictured myself with a career, but now I do. Planning social functions to raise money and awareness about these kids and other kids like them. Wouldn't that be amazing?" Her hands did as much talking as her mouth did.

"It is." Josh was staring at her the same way he had a hundred times this semester, back when she thought he was just a good friend.

If only she was sitting closer to him so that she could touch the hands that clutched his Bible. "I just feel so excited for the future instead of worried. Things are clearer than just a few days ago."

Did he know she was talking about more than just a career goal?

"Stay right there. I want to show you something." Josh flipped down from the monkey bars and ran into the guys' dorm. He came back with his sketchbook and a present wrapped in Christmas paper. He handed her the present first. "I know it's a little wrinkled. I stashed it in the bottom of my suitcase in hopes we'd be able to talk and I could give this to you."

She opened the card first. *Lansing, this is how I see you. Merry Christmas. Josh.* "Aw, that's sweet."

He walked away from the monkey bars to the nearby swings, giving her privacy to open the gift. There were drawings, all of her. On the bottom of each one, he had written the date and a title. There was one from freshman year when she and Cara had done facials on each other. He had drawn them with a pencil but colored in their green faces as they sat on the couch with popcorn. Next to the date, he wrote the title *Gossiping Giggling Girls*. Several more showed his tolerance of her through the years, but the teasing ended with the ones dated from the spring of junior year.

Then there was one from the play. She was in costume on the stage and laughing with her arms in the air. Her hair was a curly mess, but she looked so happy. He had titled it *True Beauty*. The more recent ones showed her cheering at the last game, painting in his garage, and sitting on the swing where he had confessed his feelings. Unlike the earlier ones, these were intimate, focused on her rather than the setting.

His feelings for her were in every line. How had she missed it for so long? Together, the pictures told the story of her life.

She looked up. He was staring at her. Tears slid down her cheeks, but she did nothing to stop them. He had seen her on her worst days. And still chose her. He stood firm and loyal even when she had no clue what she wanted. He waited for her to figure out her feelings for him.

He sat with his hands in his pockets, swaying slightly and waiting for her response. He had promised to wait for her, and he deserved her honesty. She tried climbing down the monkey bars, but it was hard with a handful of sketches and her journal. Just as she was going to lose the pictures, his strong hands helped her to the ground.

His arms stayed around her waist. Would he kiss her? It seemed like the perfect time, but Josh was more into the right moment than the expected one. Even if it meant waiting. "They're beautiful, Josh. You're so talented."

"Nah, the subject made it easy." He grinned and pulled her in for a hug. She leaned her head against his chest. His heart beat strong and steady. She wrapped her arms around him.

A few minutes later, she looked through the sketches again as they sat on the bench. He pulled out two more drawings from the sketchbook he had also brought out. The first one was of her at the bonfire last night. He had added colored chalk to the drawing, bringing out the gold of the fire that contrasted with the blue of her hat. "Notice the gold and blue SBU colors. Cara told me you applied."

Ellie nodded. The picture captured her mood that night. "I was so nervous at that fire. I saw you watching me, and I had so much to say but the words just wouldn't come out."

He put his arm around her and brought her close. "I'll be here whenever you're ready. Here, check this one out. I worked on this one during my painting classes with the boys."

It was a small 4x6 painting of her and Naomi. "It's amazing. I love that little girl so much." Ellie ran her fingers over Naomi's smiling face.

"I know. There were so many times I tried to get you off alone to talk about what I said. To apologize for how I acted, but she was always there. I prayed about it, realizing maybe that was part of your healing. God reminded me you were—"

"Worth the wait," Ellie finished the line. "I think I'm going to put this one in a frame if you'll let me have it."

"They're all yours. I have more."

"Oh, I want to see." Ellie leaned up, looking at him.

"You'll have to wait," Josh laughed. "It's about time you know what I go through."

Ellie's smile faded, and he hurried on. "I didn't mean that in a bad way. I was joking."

"I know." Ellie forced a smile.

"Don't give me that fake Ellie Lansing smile that fools everyone. Tell me what you're thinking." Josh set the sketches to the side and took her hands. "I can handle it."

"I was just thinking that I'm sorry I'm making you wait. I have all these emotions but can't seem to put them into words, well at least not the right words." Ellie squeezed his hand. Could he feel the words she couldn't say? "I like you, Josh, but you were right when you said that I needed to get over Dylan before moving on."

Josh's eyes lit up, and Ellie continued. "You're amazing, but my whole high school experience has been about a boy and my future with him. When I came here and saw the kids, I realized

I want to work, to have a career helping kids, instead of just being someone's girlfriend or wife."

"I would never try to tell you that's all you could be." Josh fidgeted.

"I know, and I guess what makes me nervous is that we wouldn't have some casual fling. It would be something serious. And I'm not ready for that. You deserve better. I've decided to give myself time to find out who I am, on my own." Ellie ran her fingers along his paint-flecked fingers.

Josh started to say something, but Ellie continued, "When I saw you playing with those kids, helping them paint, I was reminded of how much fun you are. When I saw you painting murals on the walls of the kids' rooms after everyone was outside relaxing, I was reminded how giving you are." Ellie cupped his face with her hands.

"You are amazing, Joshua Cole Martin, and I know a relationship with you would be more than I could even dream. And that scares me." He took her hands in his again, hauling her up to pull her into a sweet embrace.

"Thanks for telling me. That was worth the wait. You're still worth the wait," he whispered into her hair. "And I know how you feel about being scared. Why do you think I ran off the stage when it was time to kiss you?"

They strolled back to the orphanage where the kids were starting to come out to leave for school. "I think I know now."

In some ways, the last day was like all the other days, but there was a difference in the atmosphere. Throughout the day, she would occasionally look up to see Josh grinning at her in the window of the laundry room. He would jump up and down and do silly dances outside, waiting to see how long it would take for her to notice him. Her record was two minutes because she couldn't stop gazing out of the window for a glimpse of him. A few times, she stopped by to help him as he finished the last mural in the infant room. He had sketched and then painted soccer balls in the boys' room, flowers in the girls' room, and zoo animals in the nursery.

When the kids got home from school, they found the entire field full of games ready to be played. Ellie waited for Naomi, who was at the back of the group, dragging her feet. Ellie held out her arms and waited for Naomi to come running like she had every day, but she continued walking, not making eye contact with Ellie.

Ellie ran to her, sweeping her in her arms. "What's wrong?"

Naomi's face crumpled. "Don't leave, Ellie. Stay."

"Oh, I would if I could. I have to go back to school like you did today." Ellie sat down on the dirt road and held Naomi. Leaving tomorrow was going to be so hard. "But, we still have one more day of fun. Will you play with me?"

Naomi gave her a weak smile as they stood. Ellie led her to the first game. Silly String War. They each grabbed a can and joined the chaos of squeals, running, and neon-colored foam string.

Having already asked for permission, Ellie went into Naomi's room right before bedtime. Not ready to say goodbye, she picked three books the group had brought to read to the children. Too nervous to read in Spanish, she made up the story, making it as long as she could. As the little girl's eyes closed at last, Ellie spent a few minutes praying for Naomi's protection and future.

"Please, God, let me see her again, to know she's happy and healthy. And thank You for using Naomi to show me what You want me to do with my life."

The next day, Ellie had to leave Naomi behind. Everything within her wanted to take the girl home with her. Stacy and Micah needed a child, didn't they? Naomi cried through breakfast, and Ellie broke down too as they hugged one more time. She slipped the painting Josh made of her and Naomi into the little girl's hand before getting on the bus.

When they drove away, she turned in her seat. Naomi's small frame was pressed against the gate, waving until the bus was out of sight. All the girls went back to gossiping about the trip and making plans for prom, only a few months away, but Ellie flipped through pictures of Naomi on her phone. Josh sent her photo after photo that he had taken of her and Naomi with promises that she would see Naomi again. Ellie began to make a list in her journal of fundraising ideas to get another group, perhaps the youth group at her new church, to come out in the summer for a mission trip.

After filling a page with possibilities, Ellie read everything she had written about her personal journey over the last few weeks. She didn't have the rest of her life mapped out, but she was confident about the future. Because whatever God had planned for her, it would be worth the wait.

THANK YOU!

I hope you enjoyed **Worth the Wait**! I need to ask you a favor. Would you help others enjoy this book too?

Recommend it. Please help other readers find this book by recommending it to friends in person and on social media.

Review it. Reviews can be tough to come by these days. You, the reader, have the power to make or break a book. Loved it, hated it – I'd just enjoy your feedback. Please tell other readers what you thought about this book by reviewing it at one of the following websites: Amazon, Barnes and Noble, or Goodreads.

Thank you so much for reading **Worth the Wait** and for spending time with me. Above all, I hope you know how much Jesus loves you. Although life can be so hard at times, as believers we can rest in the promise that all things work together for our good. (Romans 8:28) That includes the failed dreams, the times of waiting, the heartache, and the pain. He's a good God. We can trust him. His plans are beyond anything we can imagine, and they ware worth the wait.

In gratitude,
Laura Jackson

DISCUSSION GUIDE

1. At the beginning of the story, Dylan has been distant for some time. When one of your relationships is 'off,' what do you do about it?
2. Ellie spends time straightening her hair each morning because Dylan likes it that way. Confess. Do you change something about yourself to please someone else?
3. Ellie made a commitment to not have sex before marriage. How do you hold on to your convictions?
4. Josh embarrassed Ellie by running off the stage and leaving her there alone. Have you ever been embarrassed like that? What did you do?
5. When Ellie's mom gets cancer, Ellie realizes she can't control everything. How do you handle things beyond your control?
6. Josh sends Ellie scriptures of encouragement. How can you encourage someone today?
7. When Ellie finds out Dylan cheated, she wavers between anger and grief. How do you deal with betrayal?
8. Lindsey is pretty mean to Ellie. Do you think she gets what she deserves, or do you feel sorry for her? How do you handle mean girls?
9. Dylan confesses that he felt trapped in his relationship with Ellie. Have you ever felt trapped by other people's expectations? What did you do?
10. When Ellie decides to give Dylan another chance, her brother and Josh are angry. How do you deal with friends and family who disagree with your choices? What do you do when you see a friend making a choice you think is bad, and they won't listen to you?
11. Ellie's youth group had a bonfire on New Year's Eve where they burned their list of regrets, mistakes and failures. How do you move on from your past?

RESOURCES

http://www.compassion.com
http://www.worldvision.org
Sponsor a child today through either Compassion International or World Vision.

http://www.ywam.org
Youth With A Mission: Non-denominational Christian, ministering to people around the world through evangelism, training and mercy.

http://www.yfc.net/projectserve
Project Serve is the short-term mission trip ministry of Youth for Christ.

http://www.truelovewaits.com
Make a commitment to sexual purity.

http://fervr.net
Daily Articles, Videos, Discussions for Christian Teens.

http://www.christianitytoday.com/iyf
Christianity Today site for young adults: "Ignite Your Faith." Featured articles, advice, and humor.

http://www.cdc.gov/alcohol
Center for Disease Control and Prevention: Alcohol and Public Health.

The Bare Naked Truth: Dating, Waiting, and God's Purity Plan by Bekah Hamrick Martin.

Praying for your Future Husband: Preparing Your Heart for His by Robin Jones Gunn and Tricia Goyer.

ABOUT THE AUTHOR

Laura Jackson is passionate about Jesus, books, trees, and cupcakes, in that order. She earned a Bachelor of Arts degree in English and history and fell in love with YA books while she taught 7th grade English. After earning a Master's Degree in Library Science, she became a school librarian so that she could be around books and energetic readers all day. Laura loves to hear from readers.

Email: laurajacksonwrites@gmail.com
Twitter: @laurajackson80
Pinterest: www.pinterest.com/laurajackson80
Facebook: www.facebook.com/laurajacksonwrites
Blog: www.authorlaurajackson.blogspot.com

Made in the USA
San Bernardino, CA
30 June 2018